A POISON APPLE

Also by Michel Laub

DIARY OF THE FALL

MICHEL LAUB

A Poison Apple

Translated from the Portuguese by
Daniel Hahn

Harvill *Secker*

LONDON

1 3 5 7 9 10 8 6 4 2

Harvill Secker, an imprint of Vintage,
20 Vauxhall Bridge Road,
London SW1V 2SA

Harvill Secker is part of the Penguin Random House group of companies
whose addresses can be found at global.penguinrandomhouse.com

 Penguin
Random House
UK

First published by Harvill Secker in 2017
First published with the title A maçã envenenada in 2013
by Editora Companhia das Letras, São Paulo

penguin.co.uk/vintage

A CIP catalogue record for this book is available from the British Library

ISBN 9781910701478

Typset in 12/18 pt Electra LH by Jouve (UK), Milton Keynes
Printed and bound in Great Britain by Clays Ltd, St Ives plc

Penguin Random House is committed to a sustainable future
for our business, our readers and our planet. This book is made
from Forest Stewardship Council® certified paper.

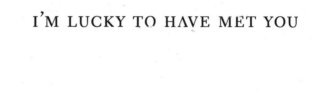

I'M LUCKY TO HAVE MET YOU

1.

A suicide changes everything its author ever said, sang or wrote. For the millions of fans of Nirvana, the band that led to his being considered the spokesman of a generation, Kurt Cobain is not a childhood in Aberdeen, the beginnings of a career in Seattle, the premature stardom that would end up changing musical history with the album *Nevermind*, nor the alcohol and the drugs and the spiral of despair followed relentlessly by the media, including the stormy marriage to the singer Courtney Love and the birth of his only child, his daughter Frances Bean. Or rather he is all these things, but only as a collection of symptoms, a mirror which, through lyrics and ill-matched accounts, reveals a scene that has never been clearly explained, at Lake Washington, April 1994, hours or days before an electrician found his body with a shotgun bullet in the head.

2.

To me, Kurt Cobain will always be the man who got up onto the stage of the Morumbi Stadium, in 1993, for what he would later call the worst show of Nirvana's career. I was living in Porto Alegre at the time, I was eighteen and in the barracks: my first shift on guard, with my first instructions for overnight duty, standing there one Thursday in front of a fat sergeant who was talking about rifle care. He couldn't say the word *password*, he'd say *pathward*, and what was the correct procedure? He would answer his own question: say halt and ask for the *pathward*.

I was in the Centre for Reserve Officer Training, known as the CPOR, the barracks assigned to those university students who'd escaped having to clean out manure in a cavalry unit or take a drubbing in the Army

Police. It didn't make much difference: I still had to submit myself to the orders of the fat sergeant, and it hardly mattered that I took sociology classes with a Jungle Warfare major, or that I attended lectures on venereal diseases and the Union budget. The 1964–85 dictatorship didn't matter either, nor did the impeachment of President Collor in 1992, nor the fact that military life in Brazil was of no interest to anyone, least of all to someone like me who lived with his parents and had a guitar and was in a band, because every morning I still had to be in my uniform at seven, with bugle and bucket and broom, and the technical name for clearing the weeds from the basketball court is *cri-cri*.

3.

I ended up at the CPOR because a friend of the family had said my name would be on a list of exemptions at the conscription bureau. But when I showed up at the desk a corporal asked my address, date of birth and whether I was at college. Law school. Where? The Federal Uni. I'd come to the end of my second semester and I was doing an internship at a nearby law firm, where I was intending to go after getting my exemption

certificate and killing some time in a café in the Public
Market. It was all planned, I even knew which tape I'd
listen to on my walkman to celebrate, but the corporal
looked for my name on the list and laughed and gave
the answer that every corporal dreams of giving to a
student with a smart shirt and leather briefcase and
headphones round his neck: so I guess it looks like
you're just going to have to defer your course.

The tape was a recording of *Nevermind*. Over the
last twenty years I may have listened to the album hundreds, possibly thousands of times, and it's as though
each time has the power to bring 1993 back: my walking out of the conscription bureau, the dirt and humidity
and a Porto Alegre summer, the noise of the buses and
a pregnant woman with a rubbish bag being followed
by a line of dogs while I stared at the document inform-
ing me that I was now under the jurisdiction of the
Army Discipline Regulations. Mine was platoon 6,
under Lieutenant Pires. There were five columns of six
men, with the tallest at the head, the others lined up
behind them in rigid single file using the back of the
neck of their fellow in front as a reference point. Thirty
students, and I haven't kept in touch with any of them.
I don't have a photo of any of them. I don't know if any

of them still lives in Porto Alegre, has children, is still alive. I might not remember anything at all that happened when we were together beyond the most general military lore, the platoon learning to march, doing moves with their guns, singing in time to the right-foot step while the company parades before the platform where the officers stand, were it not for a story that begins with Kurt Cobain coming to São Paulo.

4.

Truth is, the story really starts earlier, the night I met Valéria. I was at a bar in the Independência district, a place with a metal staircase and sweat condensed on the walls. She was my age, her mother had died when she was four, her father paid the rent on a one-bedroom apartment for her two blocks away, but those were things I only learned later because that first conversation was completely direct: they say you've got a band and you're looking for a girl to sing with you, someone who can get up there and tell everyone to go fuck themselves.

I looked at her: tattoos in the days before having tattoos was in fashion; she noticed my glass and I said, you like bad vodka? I'm a masochist, she replied. I asked how many bands she'd been in before. She asked what kind of music I listened to. I ordered another shot, she said this is our first drink together, enjoy it because it might be all downhill from here, there's no turning back now, and I kept looking at her mouth and at her hair and at the way she moved her shoulders and her hips and before I'd noticed she was pressed right up next to me.

In Valéria's apartment there was a bookcase with cassettes, band names drawn with a ballpoint pen, in a variety of characters and fonts with shading and Gothic symbols and the tips of letters made to look like lightning bolts. There was also a cat and a poster of Kurt Cobain. In the living room there was a threadbare sofa and a converted fridge used for storing books. I like old-lady décor, she said. Do you like old things? Have you ever screwed an older woman? I'm your age, but decades older than you.

Like everybody did back in the nineties, Valéria shouted when she sang. The band wasn't all that original either, arrangements that alternated between light and heavy, melody and distortion, simple four-chord bass lines of drums and bass guitar and then the guitar exploding with the three lower strings into the chorus. If you take the basic elements of *Nevermind*, the major chords, the fingerings and strummed percussive riffs, the modulating of beats and pauses and vocals reiterating the hammering percussion, you'll have the sum total of the resources we used for our songs in those first few practices. Except that Valéria had a kind of sweetness to her, even if it was restricted to her performances at the microphone, and the very first time I heard her I knew it would make a difference.

Between the night at the bar in Independência and the coming of Nirvana to São Paulo there were eleven months. Comparing the day before I met Valéria to the day after the show is like talking about different eras, worlds in opposition to one another. I've kept no photos of Valéria either, nor a single item of clothing, I didn't keep a tape with some song or other of the band's, but it's as though she were still eighteen in an eternal present, and each time I see the videos of Morumbi I know she's there, in the darkness among the first few rows, right in front of where they filmed Kurt Cobain's appearance in the middle of the blue light.

5.

Nirvana was the main attraction at Hollywood Rock, closing the Saturday-night programme after performances by Dr Sin, the Engenheiros do Hawaii and L7. Kurt Cobain was staying with Courtney Love at the Maksoud. In one report the hardcore punk singer João Gordo described the night he spent with the couple. He claimed that Courtney Love had an attack of jealousy and paid three hundred dollars to a transvestite over on Amaral Gurgel. When João Gordo complained of having a stomach ache, Kurt Cobain offered him a vial of something. The vial was kept as a trophy, and when the reporter sent it to a lab he learned that it was a treatment for heroin addiction.

During the show Kurt Cobain shouted, cried, moaned, complained, stopped several songs when they'd only just started, spat and rubbed his trousers up against the cameras. He also made a hole in one of the speakers with the neck of his guitar and fell over on the stage. At the end, he crawled off. One critic described the performance as *long, undisciplined and self-indulgent*. And he thought the most representative moment of the show was when the singer, *with a mixture of despair and doom,* destroyed all the instruments *almost delicately, beneath the silence of the audience and the stars.*

6.

During the week of Hollywood Rock, nobody at the CPOR even mentioned Kurt Cobain. Our subject was Thursday night, the first that we would be spending on a three-shift guard operation, four hours of rest after two hours attending to each of our posts: gate, backup, hillside, lateral zone and storeroom. The storeroom guard covers a large area of scrubland full of capybaras, and the fat sergeant referred to this in his preliminary briefing: you're not to shoot at every sound, it's not the little critter's fault if he's wandering around without knowing the *pathward.*

Over the course of the year a CPOR student learns to shoot a light automatic rifle, the LAR, and a 9mm pistol. At these instruction sessions we are taught basics, accuracy and safety standards. The basics are how you position your body, the way it slots into your shoulder, the lightness of your finger on the trigger until the feeling of the weapon's recoil like a shock. Accuracy is gauged relative to the sights, and a good session is one where the holes from the bullets are close to one another rather than to the centre of the target. Safety standards include loading procedure, the safety catch, getting the all-clear, and the protocol in case of weapon failure or a companion getting hit.

It was Lieutenant Pires who gave the shooting classes. In field exercises, command for the patrols always fell to an officer. The fat sergeant would, at most, spend his day at a desk overseeing the supply of fire-arms. At most, he would do deals with students who'd forgotten to return their shells, recording one mark less in the book of faults in exchange for a bag of *mate* tea and a sweet *quindim*. In his office there's a calendar, a roll of sellotape, a small basin with the Grêmio team emblem done in pyrography. On the night of our first guard duty, though, everything changes: the preliminary briefing is given in an authoritative tone of voice, by a large figure who walks about with his hands behind his back as though he were in a cross-examination. I don't want any disturbance today, the sergeant says. I haven't come out just to deal with losers. A student who keeps his nose clean will have an easy ride. Don't make me have to crap all over your life.

7.

Somebody once said that military justice is to justice what military music is to music. Life in the barracks means getting punished: there isn't a man who hasn't paid for his fellows, a whole platoon set to lug rocks because one student doesn't have a crease in his trousers, a whole company doing two hundred sit-ups in the mud because someone hasn't had his vaccination. When you're on guard duty it's even easier for this to happen, everything is recorded in the Internal Report, so the first stroke of luck you can have relates to who your companions on duty chance to be.

One of my companions that night was called Diogo. He was the one who talked most on the bench in the sentry box. He would spend the shift explaining how to fake a student card, how to throw a punch without hurting your wrist, how to get into a car with a nail and a bit of string, and it's OK, nothing's gonna happen because those Military Police are all fags, but after we heard the briefing from the sergeant Diogo didn't tell any more stories. I never heard another word out of him. We were called away by the deputy, we took our mugs and walked over to dinner, he was sitting at the next table along and we spent the whole meal avoiding each other's eye. We finished around nine thirty, returned to our quarters, then the corporal of the guard sent out the column who were to relieve the ten o'clock shift.

The earliest shift is a reasonable one compared to the others. You get to sleep three hours in a row during the night. More than for the second, which keeps watch from two to four and at five you're back on your feet for cleaning duties, or the third, which gets the worst of the cold and fog in the winter. During guard duty the students listen to music, they drink, they sleep with their arms hugged around their rifles, and one time a cavalryman was caught with a copy of the photo magazine *Sodomia*, but on my first night I spent my shift trying to concentrate, thinking about what I could and should do in the coming days.

One option was to leave the barracks on Friday, take a plane Saturday morning and be at Guarulhos airport in São Paulo by lunchtime. I'd have to cross the whole city to get to Morumbi, but that was no problem. I'd have to leave my rucksack somewhere, but that could be arranged somehow, too. I'd have to find Valéria in the middle of the crowds, ninety thousand people in Kurt Cobain goatees and flannel shirts, but even here I'd find a way. The problem was that before any of that, because of Diogo and the fat sergeant, and this was the doubt that assailed me in the storeroom, the chances were that I was under arrest.

8.

Or the story may begin somewhere else instead, on a dirt road where there are chickens, cows, a container lorry, sweet-seller stands. Gradually the landscape changes, the right-hand side of the road opens onto plantations, ibises and egrets, hippopotami and flocks of birds and antelopes and wild pigs until the vast marshes appear – the slime in the middle of the fog, the hours spent with water up over your knees and the long walks at night to find food, the first rays of sunlight and men in the distance drinking and cutting the branches just the same way you cut anything with a machete.

9.

In April 1994, engineering student Immaculée Ili-bagiza had dinner with her family in Mataba, Rwanda. With her at the table were her father, her mother, her brother and a friend who had come for the Easter holidays. Her mother talked about the harvest, her father about a grant programme from the coffee growers' cooperative, and conversation continued along these lines until her brother mentioned he had come across some Hutus carrying guns and grenades. Immaculée's family was Tutsi, the ethnicity that had been in power during the colonial period and which had been replaced by the Hutu majority following independence, in the 1960s.

Immaculée's brother had heard rumours about a kill list with the names of the Tutsi families in the area. It was nothing new in Rwanda: there had been scattered ethnic attacks right through the three decades of Hutu rule. Government radio stations compared the Tutsis to cockroaches. A song sung at schools advocated trampling them to death. All the same, the father rejected Immaculée's brother's suggestion: that they get hold of a boat, cross Lake Kivu and escape with the family to Zaire that very night.

Today Immaculée is a writer who travels the world giving talks. Recently she was in São Paulo. It was a promotional event organised by her publisher, in which she had coffee with journalists on the PUC campus, did a photo shoot and gave a lecture on what happened after the dinner in Mataba: how she helped her mother with the washing-up, then retreated to her bedroom where she prayed before a small altar she had set up with an image of Christ and the Virgin Mary. She was awoken in the small hours by her brother with the news that the president's airplane had been brought down. Immaculée leaped out of bed, put on a pair of trousers, the first time she'd ever changed clothes in front of her brother. When she opened the window she saw what looked like a yellowish halo over the village.

10.

Immaculée's father and mother were already out on the patio. The BBC read the names of the first dead on the radio. One of them was an uncle who lived in Kigali. There'd been an attempt on the prime minister. Phone lines had been cut, the highways were blockaded, and as soon as an opportunity arose Immaculée's father sent her to the house of a Hutu pastor who had agreed to hide her.

The president's death unleashed a civil war that in three months killed eight hundred thousand Tutsis, almost twenty per cent of Rwanda's population, most of them hacked to death with machetes by Hutus who had been their neighbours, their teachers, their colleagues. Foreigners fled the country in the first few days. The UN withdrew their security forces soon afterwards. There were mass rapes, decapitations, bodies left out in the open air to begin rotting before the animals ate them.

Immaculée spent those three months in a bathroom barely more than three feet square, without a sink, in the company of seven other women. The oldest was fifty-five. The youngest, seven. Any noise could give them away, they communicated in sign language, the flush could only be used when someone did the same in the toilet next door. The pastor, whose son hated Tutsis, showed up every other day with food leftovers and scraps retrieved from the rubbish. Immaculée arrived in that bathroom weighing fifty-two kilos, and left weighing twenty-nine. Her whole family, with the exception of a brother who was studying in Senegal, was killed over this period.

11.

The war in Rwanda began a day after the official death date of Kurt Cobain. I was living in London at the time. My job was to make sandwiches in a coffee shop, where I'd fill a basket, top it up with soft drinks and savoury snacks, cake and chocolate bars, to sell in the offices around Covent Garden. I didn't watch TV, I didn't buy newspapers, and half the magazines on the news-stands were written in Arabic script or were wrapped in plastic. What money I had left over from rent, transport, food and other expenses I would spend on publications about music.

I learned about Rwanda some days, maybe weeks after the event, and even then only superficially, whereas on the subject of Kurt Cobain I read everything: reporters, editors, musicians, critics and fans, in essays, statements of testimony, interviews, profiles. Everyone had something to say about his beginnings in Seattle, his debut with *Bleach* and the way *Nevermind* opened up a space on the FM stations for an aesthetic that marked punk's belated arrival into the mainstream. Everyone had something to say about the indie scene, the recording studios, the university radio stations, the clip from 'Smells Like Teen Spirit' that transformed MTV. Everyone had a verdict on Kurt Cobain, a theory about how he embodied the spirit of an age crushed by the death of utopias, about how a poorly educated generation descended into rage as they emerged from the close of the Reagan years, about what it meant to be a young person in an America overtaken by corporations, individualism and a lack of prospects, and how that was linked to this particular singer's *Via Crucis* – his dislike of fame and money, his turbulent relationship with Courtney Love, rumours about a divorce and the impending end of the band, and the heroin and the isolation that culminated in the end of the guy who would define himself as a *sad little, sensitive, unappreoiativo, Pioooo, Jooue man*.

12.

I barely heard any Nirvana in London, with the exception of the snatches of songs that started playing on the radio and in the record stores a moment after Kurt Cobain's death was announced. The news was first released by a broadcaster in Seattle, who had been notified by a friend of the electrician who found the body and said he had *the scoop of the century*. One DJ who was interviewed claimed that the singer *died a coward*. In the days that followed the funeral there were connected suicides in Seattle, in Australia and Turkey. The .20-calibre Remington that supplied the final shot was donated to Mothers Against Violence.

I read as many of these articles as I could, then after a week or two decided I didn't want to know anything further on the subject. None of my co-workers at the coffee shop did any more than say what a great shame it was. Nobody commented on the suicide note. Nobody discussed the burial or mentioned Courtney Love and Frances Bean, who was then a year and seven months old. In London in April the days are already slightly longer, the squirrels disappear, the cold stops hurting your hands and ears, on Sundays you can go to Camden and spend the morning at the market. There are records and second-hand clothes. There's a pub with a sawdust floor. You can walk in the weak sunshine up to Regent's Park, and after lunch it's almost an abstraction to think about the practicalities of death, buying a gun, choosing which room of the house you're going to take the shot in, with a kind of tiredness that has nothing in common with my sitting down to rest on a wooden bench, hollow-legged, before drinking water from a public tap and walking back between the trees and English children on roller skates.

My first instinct was to think that Kurt Cobain's motives might have been more prosaic than everything he wrote. That perhaps it was the stomach ache, something he always had with him and which he defined as being like a constant state of swallowing a live dog. I thought this not only because the pain made him use opiates and end up experimenting with heroin, from where one thing led to another: a doctor who had photos with the Rolling Stones in his surgery, a trip to the emergency room because of a thread of cotton in the syringe, the clinics, the Valium, the methadone, the ruined tours and the police and the deliberate overdose in Rome a month before the gunshot, with the pressures of the media making him feel even more beset in his exhaustion; I thought this also because the death of someone who used to be so important in your life demands an explanation that is less arbitrary.

13.

I arrived in London in January 1994, a kind of sab-
batical after the events of 1993. By the end of his time
at the CPOR a student will have done about thirty
rounds of guard duty, ninety two-hour shifts, every
minute spent thinking about what that year was and
what it might have been. For me what would most leave
its mark was that first shift of all: the conversation on
the bench in the sentry box, Diogo talking about cars
and the lamp posts a neighbour had climbed up to steal
copper wire and that one time he got pulled over and
paid the policeman with a bouncing cheque. He said
he knew how to fight with blade and chain, that once
he'd bottled a kid from the coast who almost lost an
eye, a weekend when he hid at the Tramandaí bus station so as not to be killed by the Shot-in-the-Face Gang,
and because I was the only person who laughed at his
stories, I was the one he asked about pot.

There was a story going round about a soldier in
1989 who'd been caught with his hand in someone
else's wallet. He spent thirty days sleeping in the billets,
and every morning he was woken at five, and at six he
was running, and at nine he'd already made his way up

to the exercise yard and done a set of two hundred and fifty reps of *stand-two-sit-two-stand-two. . .*, until one day he couldn't bear it any more and pointed his rifle at a corporal and his punishment went from thirty days to two years with the stroke of a pen. I don't know if it's a true story, if there's any flexibility between each barracks' inquiry procedures and if it makes any difference that the CPOR is a teaching institution and in theory more lenient. What I do know is what happened to me: the fat sergeant decided to take a walk, he passed the ramp and the path that led to the *carrière*, two posts that lit the yard, the garages and the stalls, then he turned left and returned via the engineers division and heard a noise when he reached the door to the quartermaster's hut

One cycle of guard duty is twenty-four hours without taking a bath, and you've been made to suspend your university, and the peasants laugh at you, and every morning you can smell Lieutenant Pires's foul breath as he checks your shaving with a piece of waxed paper, and so there are some nights when you realise that you don't really have all that much to lose. On one such night it's natural for you to take advantage of the break between dinner and the gathering of the overnight shift, when the barracks are deserted, before the first two hours of darkness in the storeroom, to smoke a joint with Diogo in the alley beside the changing block: the pocket of a rucksack, the plastic bag and the rizlas, a lighter and a red dot and a catching of dry grass in the silence which lasts until you are interrupted by a voice – *What's that smell, soldier?*

14.

I had left the alley a minute before the catching-in-the-act, maybe less, thirty seconds or just enough not to have been seen. I can imagine what it must have been like only from what Diogo said, with the rest of us already gathered for the overnight, with him pretending he wasn't worried and talking quietly as though that made any diffcrence: the fat sergeant appearing all of a sudden and him giving a start and then choking on the smoke or because of his nerves before he was able to say anything.

Punishments at the barracks begin with a note in the duty officer's book. The lieutenant is informed of the incident, which is published in the Internal Report. An inquiry is opened according to regular or summary procedure, a sentence handed down following the defendant making his case, or pre-emptively. The next day, Friday, at eleven o'clock, Diogo would be called to Lieutenant Pires's office to hear the official version of the words that the sergeant had spoken at Thursday's briefing, when he'd looked straight at him during the overnight instructions: any soldier who's stupid will end up learning his *pathward* behind bars.

Today I live in São Paulo, and everybody of my age claims to have seen Nirvana at Hollywood Rock, and remembers what they drank before going into the stadium, where exactly they were standing in the arena and what the order was of the songs played and what Kurt Cobain said and did in each of the breaks, even though at the time the band was in a relatively bad place with arguments, cancelled shows, rumours about hospitals and detox programmes. One report on Courtney Love claimed she had used heroin during her pregnancy. Kurt Cobain considered taking out a hit on the reporter. There were articles saying Nirvana was finished artistically, the kind of shipwreck common in the floodlit glare of that industry, the price of recording an independent debut album and eventually overtaking Michael Jackson on the *Billboard* hit parade.

But that wasn't the only reason why, on the Thursday in question, I still didn't know whether I was going to use my ticket or sell it.

The decision about whether or not to go to São Paulo would begin with the question of what Diogo was going to do to me. If he turned me in, I might be arrested that same Friday. I could be called to show up at the next overnight shift or prevented from going out even after the morning shift was done. Somebody would call my home. My mother would bring a rucksack with thirty days' worth of clothes. That would be the period I would be sleeping in a cell, or perhaps in the billets, and at most I'd be allowed to receive visitors on Sundays, and I was sure Valéria would not be among them.

15.

Or alternatively a different setting. A city that isn't yours, but which looks so very familiar. A street with wide pavements. A man dancing on his own. A man announcing the end of the world. You walk up to the entrance to the building, there's a lady standing in line, the girl on the till. A few coins in change and the stamp with the face of a princess from a hundred and fifteen years before. The correspondence travelling across space and time. Towards an address you also know. And you know what will happen when the order you've placed reaches its destination.

16.

I was the last person off the plane when we arrived in London. The city was almost dark at half past three in the afternoon, and the first thing I saw from the train leaving the airport was the suburbs, identical house after identical house as far as the horizon. I had enrolled in an English course to try and get myself a student visa. I dropped out in the second week and started looking for work. There was an agency in a Brazilian restaurant in Notting Hill. I got myself a casual job handing out flyers in Bethnal Green. Each day I would travel to one part of the neighbourhood with ads for carpets, plumbers, dry-cleaning, and until I got my job in the coffee shop I also covered the breaks for a Polish man at a baked potato place. I also did the cleaning in a three-storey house in Islington, five pounds plus a bus pass and a plate of chilli.

I wore the same jacket for months, the same trousers and the same boots. I shared a room in a hostel
with a Spaniard. We used the same travelcard because
he worked night shifts and I worked during the day: I'd
wake up around six, it was about forty minutes to get to
the coffee shop. Queensway, a change at Holborn and
one stop to Covent Garden: I'd open up the shop, have
some tea, make the sandwiches, dozens of them and
with the exact amount of filling, bacon and avocado,
chicken and sweetcorn, egg and prawn, then I'd serve
customers at the café and go out with the basket to sell
in the offices. I worked around twelve hours a day. I
earned three pounds an hour, which was the price of a
smoked salmon bagel and a Sprite. Weekly rent was
sixty. A cinema ticket, depending on the place and the
time of day, was four, six or eight.

17.

The owner of the coffee shop owed money to his
suppliers, to the owner of the building, to his employ-
ees. My own credit never fell below two hundred
pounds. I noted down all payments in a little diary,
along with telephone numbers and comments on the

coffee shop. It was a kind of journal that today allows me to see precisely what I did on the day Kurt Cobain died, and what I did in the weeks that followed, too. Also what I did the rest of the time I spent in the city: the bits of slang I used half a dozen times, the places I went to half a dozen times, the people I spoke to half a dozen times and whose names I would forget immediately afterwards.

I wrote nothing in the diary about Brazil. There was no internet, phone calls were expensive, I spent months without reading a newspaper or magazine in Portuguese. Sometimes I'd make a reverse-charge call to my parents, I sent my first and last card very soon after arriving, and two or three times I went to the job agent's restaurant to eat black beans and spring greens followed by a condensed milk sweet. I had never spent so much time on my own. There was no one in London who knew a thing about me. Inevitably it occurred to me that I could change address and job and spend years incognito, and my name would only be heard again if I died and they found my passport and the embassy tracked down my family. There's not a word in the diary about that almost total feeling, which sometimes alarmed me because all you have to do is stretch your freedom out to its furthest extent and from one moment to the next you no longer have a past, there's nothing you miss because it's as though nothing has happened, or only the things you've chosen, those memories that are good and inoffensive, and nothing you did or said to a person has any consequence because you never have to meet them again, or think of them, or imagine and confront what became of them in another time and on another continent in a life that sometimes doesn't seem even to have belonged to you.

18.

I haven't had many relationships between 1993 and today, at least not the long ones that end up serving as a point of comparison for the others. It's as though the night I met Valéria was the starting benchmark, and from the chance occurrence of my arriving at her house and seeing the Kurt Cobain poster and her commenting that her biggest dream ever was to see a Nirvana show, a wave of premonition arose that contaminated all the conversations and fights and getting-back-togethers and break-ups I would have over two decades.

Valéria was the first girlfriend I had. At fourteen

I asked a schoolmate who would come to be known as Nail – as in fingernail – to ask another schoolmate called Sandra what she thought of me. Everything was set up for a birthday party and I had prepared just what I was going to say. I went so far as to stand in front of the mirror to practise my lines and how I'd hold my shoulders, in a denim jacket and checked deck trainers, but once there I just leaned against the wall and waited for the right moment to ask her to dance. I promised I'd do it during the next song, and at that moment Sandra was chatting to a girlfriend. Then the next song came along, and she was getting up to go to the bathroom. The hall was on the ground floor with a glass door opening to the garden. People came in and out and there was one moment when there we were, the two of us, me and Sandra in opposite corners – her not looking directly at me and perhaps waiting for me to take the initiative – when Nail sat down beside her.

I'd been a classmate of Nail's since nursery school. Not long before the party he'd been going around with his tracksuit bottoms spattered with glue and saying look, there's cream coming out. In a cookery class he'd been on the dessert team and said he'd filled a cake with his own pubic hairs. Nail told us about how he'd hidden in the girls' bathroom and spent the morning spying on people through the slit of a cubicle, and because of the angle of the mirror he'd been able to check out whose ass was saggy, and who took a peek at whose breasts. When he said something in Sandra's ear and she began to laugh and he said something else and she laughed again I knew that very quickly the hall would be empty, with only the two of them on the dance floor, the music playing loud and the lights from the disco ball and her face level with his chest, and when I saw the two of them again they were glued nose to nose.

19.

I met Valéria when I was eighteen, and since Nail and Sandra's dance I'd had little chance to do any more than drink and sniff benzene at all the parties in all the clubs in Porto Alegre where I ended up sleeping in a wet bathroom, or yelling at the loudspeaker, and there's always someone putting you in a cab and giving the address and the driver grumbling OK but he'd just better not mess up the seat cos I only cleaned that shit up today. If I hadn't played guitar since I was a kid, and later bought an electric guitar, a reverb pedal and a fuzzbox, and spent my whole time copying every chord and the tonality of every bootleg show and B-side and rare recording I managed to get my hands on from a seller nicknamed Tape-Guy, it's quite possible that I would still be doing the same to this day.

I had my first band when I was twelve. The drum kit was a snare, a cymbal and a tupperware box that Nail used as a floor tom. The first gig we played was also at a birthday party, five songs with lyrics attacking the school headmistress and Brazil's rampant inflation. The band came to an end more or less at the time of the dance with Sandra, more or less for that reason, though I never discussed it with Nail and he never again took Sandra's hand like he did that night, the two of them walking out of the party hall towards the garden, with me leaning up against the wall for how much longer, five minutes, ten minutes, until I could leave without saying goodbye and without anyone asking any questions or hearing the story of what had happened.

That party was in November. Term ended in December. My family had a beach house and I wouldn't be seeing my schoolmates again until March. It was the year that surfing came into fashion, and when school started again everyone had waxed hair, bowl cuts, seagull-print shirts and rubber wallets and flipper-shaped key rings. I had never had a surfboard, I'd never liked the beach, and I barely went into the water in those three months in which I would wake up late and spend the day in my room on my guitar with the volume off. It was a wooden house, fifty degrees even after two o'clock in the afternoon, and I spent the years that followed writing and singing and recording all on my own, songs I showed nobody until I met Valéria.

20.

One of the songs we used to play with Valéria was a cover of 'Drain You'. She asked for the pacing to be slower and she sang in an ironic tone that would later become common with Richard Cheese and others. Her talent was obvious, and two minutes into the first practice it was clear that the band would depend on the vocals, but this feeling may have been due to the fact that no woman like her had ever come close to me before. It's hard to assess someone like Valéria, at least to begin with, because beauty is an obstruction that makes us look at whoever's standing at the microphone as though the rest of the band doesn't exist, or the rest of the world.

My first time was with Valéria. I was eighteen and I must have been the only virgin of my age. At fourteen Nail went with a gang of schoolmates to a whorehouse close to the school, an old building on Venâncio Aires from which I fled the moment a fish-faced lady opened the door. Everything I knew about the subject was limited to the movies and magazines and the lies it's easy to tell: you just say an uncle took you back to the old house a while later, and that time you didn't forget your money or have an urgent appointment, you can even describe the bedroom, the fish-faced lady's clothes, her lipstick and her scales, because Nail told the story so many times it's only natural to retain the details. Except that it all changes when it's real, when I accept one more glass of vodka at Valéria's place, and the conversation about the Kurt Cobain poster gives way to silence, then she pulls me into the bedroom, it's hot and she turns on the fan and draws back the sheet, a cover that heaps up at the foot of the bed, and there's a lit candle and I take off my shirt and she pulls me towards her again and says be careful there's a chance I might like it.

They say nobody forgets that moment, the intensity

and the relief and the gratitude at discovering how simple it is, all you need to do is to allow Valéria to rest her chest up against yours, and her waist, and the rest happens practically on its own, practically a miracle. From then on you're a different person because you were able to put your hand on her stomach and lower yourself down, an instinctive movement as you get used to the expression on her face beginning to contort, and I close my eyes and keep on going and it's the best memory I have as she says hoarsely, are you really sure? You really know what you're letting yourself in for? Look at me, Valéria says: are you really ready to go all the way?

21.

'Drain You' is the eighth track on *Nevermind*, and the idea of doing a cover came from that very first night, the conversation we were having next to the poster. Valéria asked if I spoke English, if I'd ever paid any attention to Kurt Cobain's lyrics, if I'd spotted the themes of abuse in 'Polly', of religion in 'Lithium', the bridge metaphor in 'Something in the Way', if I'd noticed the line that talks about the biblical fruit of knowledge that brings freedom and damnation.

I listened to 'Drain You' hundreds of times, both before and after that conversation, and there was no other song in which the usual progress of a Kurt Cobain composition, fragmented lines with echoes of stories and feelings that the fans sensed or knew from other sources, all sufficiently vague as to acquire whatever meanings one chose for them, had so much impact. The image projected by the singer was of someone trying to resist the pressures of the record companies, of the press and the public, and everyone does or doesn't believe the suicide was a response to all that, but to me the idea of purity will always be associated with the simplicity of those lyrics, an intimate subject with no political resonance or reference to the market, the scene of two children or a couple saying to each other how lucky to have met you. I don't care what you think, unless it's about me. The water is so yellow, you're my vitamins. Chew your meat for you, pass it back and forth in a passionate kiss.

22.

'Drain You' was one of the songs I listened to most in the CPOR storeroom, eleven months after my first conversation with Valéria. My walkman was hidden in my trousers, the cable pulled up between the buttons of my military jacket, and even their first time on guard there aren't many students who follow the sergeant's advice about how important it is to concentrate on your work. When I reached my post I sat down and put on my headphones. The storeroom is where the munitions and gunpowder are kept and if anyone had wanted to turn me in and open the door and strike a match and send the barracks sky-high there would be nothing I could do to stop them.

In the first weeks at the CPOR all I wanted was to be discharged. All I needed was a back problem, a bit of paper certifying a murmur or an arrhythmia, or a hammer and my fingers broken so I couldn't use my rifle. Every day I'd think about this as I left the house, watching myself from above as I left the house wearing my out-of-barracks uniform, my watch synchronised to Lieutenant Pires's, today is the day I march-and-do-the-weeding-and-lunch-on-egg-and-a-chicken-carcass-floating-in-fat for the last time: there's nothing they can do but classify me as a deserter, and at worst I'd have a stamp on my file and I wouldn't be able to enter the competition to join the civil service. When I shared the joint with Diogo that was what was in my mind – what am I doing here, why do I have to be here at the age of eighteen, having got through one of the most difficult college entrance exams in the state of Rio Grande do Sul? I have a band and an internship and I'm sitting here in my cap with a gun in my hand protecting a poor barracks against an enemy that has never existed. If you asked what I'd do if I got caught, whether in the changing block or on guard duty, whether smoking pot or listening to music in the storeroom, I'd have told you that a month of prison followed by dismissal from the army might not actually be such a bad deal.

23.

And at the same time it wasn't easy. I didn't know any doctors who could provide a certificate. Not everyone has the courage to inflict an injury on himself. Fear is a feeling with a life of its own, independent of what you imagine could be the worst eventuality in a particular situation: what could happen if something went wrong in the storeroom, what could be worse than Diogo's accusation, why should I be nervous about spending two hours with a rifle in my hand surrounded by trees that seemed like living giants in the gloom, the wind and the leaves swaying, a branch that fell down a few metres away as soon as I took off my headphones because I started thinking about Diogo and that something was wrong, a howl, a moan and someone seeming to call me soldier, soldier, and you forget the previous day and the following week, and all that matters is finishing your shift safely.

In the army you get used to being grateful for small things. All it takes is a rota that has left you with a free weekend. All it takes is an inspection by the colonel who mentions the cleanness of the yard, a compliment on your performance as sheriff of the group, and the morning goes on and football time arrives and one more class till lunch and the surprise of being let out earlier than usual at two in the afternoon. Every time I left the barracks meant one day less, and it didn't matter whether it was January or February, March or April, the feeling was always the same when I passed the sentry box and took the bus into Borges de Medeiros. The Marinha Park, the tabebuia trees and a piece of the Guaíba River, the clean sky and me in my dark glasses and the rest of the day free like I hadn't had in weeks, and remembering what I could do in each of these precious minutes helped to increase the doubt about prison: the prospect of a month sleeping in the barracks, the toilet without a lid and the same clothes and the food and the louse-infested mattress, thirty days painting walls and scrubbing the floor and carrying sacks of cement with three companies and six platoons and two hundred students and more soldiers and corporals and sergeants and officers who will never forget your story.

If Diogo shopped me to the lieutenant, I would forever be soldier number 688, platoon 6, who got caught during his very first stint on guard duty. Two hundred people making comments about the case in the universities and bars of Porto Alegre. A law student at the Federal University of Rio Grande do Sul who took drugs inside the barracks. Who was stupid enough to act as described in Diogo's account, a legal case with the testimony of sentries who heard the conversation between the two defendants on the bench in the sentry box, him asking if I smoked, kidding around about what it would be like to do it in the barracks, the overnight shift and the superior officer's rounds, and me saying I had a joint and we could go to the billets and take a hit if he'd pay me back with a beer or in actual money.

24.

Valéria left on the Tuesday before the Nirvana show. The bus takes eighteen hours between the Porto Alegre bus station and the Tietê terminal in São Paulo. She stayed in the house of an aunt she hadn't seen since she was a child, and when she arrived on the Wednesday it was just as it usually is in São Paulo: the smell of carrion on the riverside highway, the bridges and churches, the bulldozers and air vents, the capybaras and the sofas dumped in the sewers. Her aunt drove them to her building in Santana, explained that from there to Morumbi there was at least an hour's traffic, and that on the way out of the show there wouldn't be any transport and the cost of a taxi could be half as much as the intercity coach ticket including the dinner near Florianópolis, the afternoon snack in Curitiba and breakfast in Registro.

When they arrived at the house, her aunt showed her the guest bedroom, the bathroom, the kitchen and the utility room. She handed her a copy of the key and said there was a cake in the oven. I don't remember where this aunt worked, if she had a husband, if she was her mother's sister or cousin or her father's or some other relative of Valéria's. I don't know if she still lives in São Paulo, and if she retained the conversation that happened at the table, around the coffee cups and the crumbs, if Valéria used a knife and fork or held the cake in a napkin, if they talked of the city and the aunt's life or about Porto Alegre, the apartment, the band she sang in and what was going to happen to the band after the Nirvana show.

25.

I don't know if Valéria told her aunt she had a boyfriend. If she mentioned her boyfriend's name, how old he was and where she'd met him. If she also remembered the first night, the dim light in her bedroom and the humming of the fan, and what she meant when she asked if I was ready to go all the way. I don't know if on the night before the Nirvana show she remembered having used those words, in that exact order, if it was a request or a warning or just what you do if you've been drinking vodka and your voice is hoarse in my ear now and you say go all the way and I heard it as though I was used to it.

I was the first to wake up the next day. I remember

noticing the position she was sleeping in, all her weight on her arm, the pillow under her neck and the pacified expression she had so rarely. It's very hard to see beyond the beauty, all the more so on the first morning of the first relationship: Valéria said I should stay in bed, she returned with a tray of juice and biscuits, I just watched the way she ate, how she stretched, our first kiss in natural light, her body in detail now – her toes, her knees, the colour of her skin.

What's the worst thing you can discover about someone? The first days went by without Valéria having a psychotic attack, or revealing that she'd spent years in prison, or that she believed in a theory about reptilian creatures that had secret meetings to control the world, so there were plenty of conversations that were strange or not, to be taken seriously or not, with Valéria laughing as she asked me if I'd still be there if she were cross-eyed. If she were missing a leg. If she took off her clothes and I discovered a scar running down from her collarbone to her waist and her back covered in knife marks and cigarette burns.

From time to time Valéria would ask if I'd ever taken care of anyone. If I'd made any sacrifices in my life. A *real* sacrifice, she'd say, though I don't know why that kind of conversation should have worried me. It's as if those first weeks were an accident, a time capsule in which she happened not to show anything that made me back sensibly away before I'd got myself involved in something that could not be undone. I remember the first practice I took Valéria to, what it was like to play in the band with my girlfriend, each meeting where we discussed the lyrics, the arrangements, and in each of these memories I try to identify a word or gesture or expression that might have alerted me to what eleven months later would start to look with hindsight like a fatal act – the way she behaved towards the drummer, who was the only survivor of the old band from school, my one-time classmate Nail who took the trip with Valéria to São Paulo.

26.

I've liked music since I was a kid. According to my mother, when I was three or four years old my favourite toy was a xylophone. My father used to listen to the university radio, I remember the hissing of the orchestra recordings, the announcer who would appear with his serious voice saying names I thought were funny,

bassoon, andante, trombone. At six I began guitar lessons, and the hard thing at first is to hold the strings
down for long enough, shape a B-minor barre chord
before you've got the calluses on your fingers and
strength in your wrist, then the right hand, the finger-
ing, and later the plectrum and the solo scales.

I started to like rock music in the 1980s. I'd spend
my afternoons listening to Ipanema FM, recording and
noting down the names of tracks in a little book in
which I would try to reproduce lyrics and chord charts.
The first gig I saw was in the Araújo Vianna auditorium, and what struck me the most was the volume of
the instruments and how much older Marcelo Nova
looked than in the photos on his record. I followed all
their careers, Fabião from Olho Seco, Redson from
Cólera, Clemente who was accused of having betrayed
the movement, and even though I attended private
school and had a maid who brought me mid-afternoon
toasted cheese sandwiches and milkshakes, I was
deluded into believing I was very close to the world in
which these people lived.

No one in my class knew how to play. No one knew
the first thing about music. I hated my classmates' taste,
their clothes, their slang, all the surfer videos and those

Australian bands that you saw driving sports cars with women in bikinis, with those haircuts and dark glasses and bronzed vocalists who revealed their perfectly aligned teeth beneath the blue sky, while Nail and I spent our weekends playing in the garage of his house among tools and tins of paint and the sticky humidity that smelled of cement and dog.

27.

Nail listened to the same things as me: Californian skate punk bands, bands of skinheads from Holland, Santa Claus the capitalist whore who gives to the rich and spits on the poor. He was the only person in school with any sense of rhythm, thirty students in my class and thirty in B and C classes, the same in the year above and the one below and only he was capable of something as simple as coordinating his legs and arms. In those days there was nothing like playing with accompaniment: a three-in-one hi-fi that makes the snare vibrate, a Tonante guitar, the scratchy wailing that transforms the world into a cough like ground glass.

Music was also the reason Nail was my best friend.

After the incident of the dance with Sandra we were estranged for a while, but by the final years of high school we had already made our peace. On Fridays we'd go down to Osvaldo Aranha, he started on coke and acid and one time he took the girlfriend of a goth into Redemption Park. That was when he got his nickname: I'm not going to have a bath for a week, he said, holding up his finger, you can smell her under this nail. He was the first person to mention Kurt Cobain, appearing with a tape of *Bleach*, one of the last albums of the eighties and a recording that was traditional and new at the same time.

The critics used to say *Bleach* was a rehearsal for what a mixing tub and a subtle adjustment of tempi, together with the market transformation that came to embrace the standard formulas of the American indie scene, would transform two years later into *Nevermind*. In this period I concluded my third year, passed my college entrance exam, under the common misconception that there is a vocation in what is merely the triumph of concentrated study, and by the first of my university classes was already beginning to realise I could indeed become a lawyer, or compete to become a judge, or become the calmest and most stable employee on a labour arbitration board, or anything that would give me the support that a music class and a life of alcohol and a percentage of the cover charge in twenty-person bars would never give me, but what I really wanted was to go back to having a band.

28.

Nail bought a ticket to go with me and Valéria to Nirvana weeks before we had any idea how we were going to get there. Neither of them had the money for the plane trip, but I was going to have to figure something out there because I couldn't predict what Friday and Monday in the barracks were going to be like. Eighteen hours' travelling there and eighteen hours back, between two working shifts that might be bureaucratic or might include a twelve-kilometre march with helmet and haversack, and all this well before the episode with the pot and Diogo, was not perhaps the ideal option.

I avoided telling Valéria I couldn't guarantee being able to go, that it was perfectly possible that I'd be absent for the most important moment of her life, the moment she'd been talking about so much and for so long, and with the hindsight of fate it wouldn't be hard to identify this as one of the points of conflict. There were nights when I didn't meet her because the following morning I'd have to be at the barracks early. Weekends when I was too tired to do anything but sleep. Conversations where I couldn't stick to any subject other than the trap into which I had fallen, eighteen years old and suddenly living in slavery, and nobody could understand how the shine of a buckle and a collar pin and the precise length of a shoelace had come to be so important, and every time I fretted about it almost to tears of rage Valéria would ask so what was stopping me from just deserting? What's the worst thing that could happen, you'll be sent to the firing squad? You won't be able to renew your voter registration, is that it?

29.

It would be easy enough to say that that was how the problems with Valéria started, a classic storyline of a girlfriend not getting enough attention. And then the hindsight of fate returns to that first practice session, the way Nail greeted her, the way he started to behave towards her in the weeks that followed and her comments about how nice and devoted and sensitive he was. You remember the way she stood as she sang, the way she moved her body knowing that she was always being watched from that angle; I don't know if those movements were unconnected to the fact Nail was there or if it happened naturally – a question she asked him, her voice quieter, the first time he held her gaze, the day she held his gaze right back while I was on the other side of the garage changing a string or sorting out a plug with a faulty contact.

I never learned the details of what happened in the days leading up to the Nirvana show. I don't know if Valéria's aunt asked whether Nail wanted to sleep in the living room or the guest bedroom. I don't know where he ended up sleeping, what he said to Valéria, what he did with her or didn't do up until the moment Kurt Cobain stepped onto the stage, three days in which they were alone amid millions of people who didn't know about them or have any interest in them, a period I was only able to reconstruct from Nail's subsequent account: what Valéria ate in Florianópolis, Curitiba and Registro, their arrival and the Tietê Riverside, the walks on Paulista and in the city centre, Thursday and Friday and Saturday in which she remembered me or didn't, wanted to get in touch with me or didn't, decided or did not decide to explain to me what I was never able to understand.

30.

The person who killed Immaculée Ilibagiza's parents was a businessman called Felicien, whose children had been classmates of hers at primary school. She visited him in prison after the end of the war. His skin was damaged, he had wounds all over his feet, a filthy beard. Felicien set fire to Immaculée's house, he stole pieces of machinery and the grain harvest. When he saw her at the door to his cell he began to cry. The prison warden said that she could question him, she could kick him and spit on him if she wanted.

Historians explain the Rwanda genocide as the consequence of a rivalry between Tutsis and Hutus that pre-dated colonial times. Even though it was hard to distinguish one ethnicity from the other, not least because of the decades of intermarrying that produced children with mixed features, the Belgians encouraged a policy of segregation based on different ID documents and quotas in the political and educational systems. In addition to this there were the episodes of civil war in the second half of the twentieth century and, finally, a series of cases of negligence: on the part of the UN, who did not intervene adequately when the massacres began, and of institutions such as the World Bank and the IMF, who failed to oversee the resources from charities which were used, for example, for the mass production of machetes.

Immaculée often talks about her experiences from a Catholic perspective. Her lectures are preceded by clips and advertisements that designate her the Anne Frank of Rwanda. In her autobiography she says the killers allowed the Devil to take charge of their souls. That she spent the ninety-one days in the bathroom praying. That she held on to a rosary given to her by her father the last time they'd seen each other. On her visit to the prison, she says she could see Felicien's shame and that, when their eyes first met, she too had been unable to control her tears. Then she put her hand on his shoulder and, in a scene she described often in her lectures, her voice cracking with emotion, explaining that if she had not done this she would never be able to love and trust people again, or, as she defines it, *to continue being human,* she said she forgave him.

31.

I interviewed Immaculée early last year, after her talk at PUC, a freelance job for a magazine that ended up being published with some cuts and changes. I've been a journalist since 1995. When I returned from London my place at law school had been suspended, I no longer had my internship at the law firm and until the new year of classes began I stayed home. The only thing I could think to do was to type the information from my English diary into the computer. Taking advantage of how easy it was to swap around paragraphs, insert new passages and redraft sections, in two months I printed out the final version of what would be a kind of book about my trip. The results are amateur, with saccharine passages and insistent musings on the history and day-to-day lives of a country in which I'd lived for less than a year, but it was enough for my mother to send it to a friend whose daughter was married to a journalist in São Paulo. I soon began sending pieces of writing to the magazine where he worked, then to other publications, and the editor of one of these invited me to work for him two years later.

32.

As a journalist I was more of an editor than a reporter, though I always did enjoy doing interviews, and in neither one of those functions did I ever experience anything like my meeting with Immaculée. I attended the lecture at PUC and we went together, by car, on a rainy day in slow traffic, to the smart hotel in the Jardins where she was staying. We took a seat in the lobby and I switched on my tape recorder. She was wearing a suit, she was made up, she was thirty-nine and she was pleasant throughout.

Immaculée spoke about her husband, she told me what she'd said when her daughter asked about her grandparents, about her daughter's reaction when she saw her mother on a TV programme which was intercut with studio commentary and scenes from 1994, the bellies of women pregnant after having been raped, HIV-positive Hutus whose task was to contaminate Tutsi teenagers, bodies hanging from trees and surrounded with flies whose buzzing was louder than the engines of the jeeps, a country whose image would come to be framed by the cameras of CNN, the lettering of the subtitles on the screen, the numbers lost to ethnic cleansing and the razed earth and time stopping.

One of the questions I considered asking her was about a report by Jean Hatzfeld, the testimony of a woman who felt ashamed at having survived. To talk about it, the woman said, is to demean oneself in others' eyes. It is to allow others to speculate about what you might have done to have escaped, why you were spared, the cases of accusations and people who left children behind and hid themselves in corpse-filled ditches. How is one to avoid one's memories being mixed up with guilt, with self-pity and self-indulgence in the years and decades that come after such an event? How is one to hold a tape recorder and look at a person and bring up these things after she has spent ninety-one days in a bathroom while her family was dismembered right out in the open?

33.

One of the questions I did ask Immaculée was about the doubts that arose in the bathroom. She says in her book that she prayed in silence, moving her mouth because this distracted her from what she must not hear, the voice of the Devil whispering you are only one, your enemies are legion, why ask for help from the God who sent your whole family to die?

During the ninety-one days she spent there, Immaculée kept in fragmentary contact with the news about the war. The pastor positioned a wardrobe in front of the bathroom door, a disguise to prevent the constant patrols from finding the hideaways, and yet it was still possible to hear what the house's residents and visitors were saying. That was how Immaculée heard her Hutu boyfriend playing volleyball, joking with his friends, drinking beer and praising the prolonged, generous meals. That was how she learned that her brother, one of the few people in the province to have completed a master's course, had had his skull split open by a Hutu who wanted to know what the brains of *such a clever little cockroach* looked like. One day the pastor appeared early in the morning and, predicting that the eight women would be the only Tutsis left in Rwanda, that he would be killed if they told anyone about their hiding place, and because of this that they should go somewhere no one knew them, predicting this he remarked that he would soon be sending them to the island of the Abashi – a tribe with no schools, churches or houses nor any contact with the outside world, where the men lived by hunting and fishing and with any luck the women would be taken on as their wives.

During the ninety-one days, Immaculée had a fever, lice and a urinary infection, her skin flaking and her gums sore, and trouble sitting up on the floor because she had lost the muscle tone and fat in her body. Whenever the Hutu patrols surrounded the house she felt the physical sensation of fear, the burning scalp, her back as though pricked by needles, sweat, headaches, a tightening of her chest, the floor seeming to move because of her constant, uncontrollable tremors, and at these moments she would close her eyes and concentrate on a mantra, spending hours thinking only of this, sometimes just a single word of comfort, *faith, hope, deliverance*, even after everything had returned to peace and quiet.

34.

Every day Immaculée gave thanks for the pastor's house having been built, for the architect having remembered to make an extra bathroom, for the bathroom door that was narrow enough to be concealed by the wardrobe. She selected a passage from the Bible, usually some verses from the Gospel of Mark, and repeated over and over that God reveals only that which we are ready to understand. God reveals only what we need. God can do all things for all people, and any normal person is as well protected as Daniel in the lion's den.

Immaculée talked about what she felt in the first days, her desire to kill the Hutus, and how she had to deal with this in each conversation she had with Tutsis after the end of the war. She needed to understand her anger. She needed to confront it, to overcome it, and even in the bathroom she began to pray for everyone – victims, killers, those who had done good and done evil in those three months of apocalypse. What she discovered was the proof that being spared was not the same as being saved, and there is more to be done than to lament the gratuitous horror, the cycle that from our birth to our death is a test of our ability to bear pain and acceptance.

I switched the tape recorder off after the interview, thanked her for the time she had spent with me, got a taxi outside the hotel and then arrived home. I had a

glass of water. I took off my shoes. I turned off the bedroom light and decided to lie down for a little. I had
twenty-four hours to write up the piece, I still had facts
that needed checking and the recording to transcribe,
and I remember thinking it would be best to make a
start at once and type up as many chunks of text as possible to arrange them the next morning and not think
about what I had just seen and heard, about what had
happened since I had said goodbye to Immaculée – a
feeling I had but didn't know if it was because of her or
because of the coincidence of dates or because I had
barely thought about it all in twenty years, Rwanda and
London, 1994 and 1993, Kurt Cobain and the CPOR
and Nail and Valéria, and I didn't know how such a
brief conversation with someone I'd never met before
had the power to affect me this way.

35.

I went into law school because I liked watching
courtroom dramas. Also because I thought it was possible to chase criminals without breaking a sweat or
rumpling your suit. Also because they said I'd go hun-
gry if I became a musician. Except that after two

months of college I had already realised I wouldn't be able to concentrate for more than half an hour on reading things that were only going to get worse: commercial law, agrarian law, welfare law, court procedure and juridical hermeneutics, six years in which I would pay attention to no more than half a dozen subjects and do the rest by cheating from summaries secreted in the legal codes.

My internship at the law firm began in the first term. The work was equivalent to that of an office boy: retrieval of papers relating to a lawsuit at the Fórum, photocopying rulings at the courthouse, procedural questioning for the expert in the employment suit filed by Geová the boiler supervisor – *did the firm comply with all the requirements of safety legislation?* I earned half the basic minimum wage for working from one till six thirty, classes were at night-time, and I paid for my college snacks and clothes and beers in addition to the amplifier I bought in ten instalments because I hadn't received an allowance since leaving school. I topped my earnings up as best I could: taking the bus and telling the firm I'd gone by cab; typing up pieces of student work which were paid by the page; a party where we charged admission and kept the takings on the bar; the pot that a fellow law student got hold of for me to resell.

In the conversation with Diogo sitting on the bench in the sentry box, the first person to mention pot was not me. Technically I didn't sell it to him, because a transaction presupposes an agreement about the quantity and the price and I didn't even make an offer, just a comment that was almost a courtesy, a joke, you buy me a beer or pay it into my account later. Needless to say, he never paid me the money, and for the amount involved it was a risible sum, and every one of the two hundred students and the corporals and sergeants and lieutenants and majors and who knows perhaps even the colonel were already tired of smoking or cohabiting with people who smoked pot, but this would not take away the fact that there is a difference between using narcotics and dealing in them.

36.

At the moment Diogo was caught, I was walking over to the billets. It was about twenty minutes before we saw each other again at the start of the overnight shift. During that time I don't know what Diogo did, whether the fat sergeant left the alley immediately after saying that he would be arrested, that he should get ready to take cold showers for thirty days, eat animal feed for thirty days, sleep thirty days knowing that on the thirty-first he would be expelled with the stamp of pothead on his file.

Perhaps Diogo remained where he was, sitting there, him and the steamed-up windows of the changing block next door, the smell of smoke still in the air and the hangover of realising what had just happened, or perhaps he walked round to the back of the engineers division and for a moment considered jumping the wall and running away forever. I don't know exactly how it happened, but it was during this time that he decided, and it is sometimes more like a quick realisation, an instinct when you're at bay and apparently have no way out, that he couldn't not react.

Diogo came over to talk to me as soon as I was out of the billets. He said he had tried to deny that he'd been smoking. That the fat sergeant had made him spread his legs and raise his arms. Everything in the army is ceremonial, you're trained so that by the second month you stop feeling strange when you take off your cap in enclosed places, when a superior comes in and you have to get to your feet, standing to attention when you reply to someone who has a torch and is checking over the floor of the alleyway and through the earth of the flower beds until they find the tip of the joint: what's this, soldier? I don't know, sergeant, sir. Does this soldier think his sergeant is an idiot? I don't think that, sergeant, sir.

When he came to the CPOR Diogo thought that he would go through basic training, the long working shifts and the field exercises, and sometime around the middle of the year things would calm down. He only had one guard shift every ten days, some possible duties as assistant to the adjutant or the duty sergeant, half a dozen tests in the few months until graduation. Then it would be an internship as an officer-to-be somewhere in the interior, a promotion when he came out. An ex-student can opt for up to eight years as a second-grade lieutenant after his compulsory service, with an officer's salary and subsidised housing and a healthcare plan for his family, but prison changed everything: he'd do the thirty days and he would be cut off, labelled a criminal for the rest of his life, a scapegoat who would agree to remain quiet in the name of a gratuitous loyalty, and so I was going to have to pay if I didn't want to be taken with him.

BEYOND THE BEAUTY

37.

One explanation for what happened in April 1994; Kurt Cobain had a wife, a daughter one year and seven months old, the money and fame to do successfully just what he had always enjoyed doing, as well as the option of giving this up at any moment and living however he chose, far from the press, the audiences, in any city he wanted, in a house he could get built for him, surrounded by the people he liked and with decades of material comfort ahead of him, and yet he still pulled the trigger. Whereas Immaculée Ilibagiza went into a three-foot-by-four bathroom and spent ninety-one days eating the leftovers brought by the pastor, sleeping and using the toilet in front of seven other women, and seeing the other seven doing the same, each one's noises and her metabolism, a rota of who stood and who slept and who cried and who fell ill, and during that time she knew or imagined she would lose her house, her city, her country, her language, her family and all the reference points that make a person who she is, but at no time did she ever contemplate anything but survival.

38.

One explanation for why I was in London in the week Immaculée went into the bathroom and Kurt Cobain killed himself: a car accident I had had the year before. I crossed Protásio Alves, at a traffic light opposite the bus lane, and a fire engine ran into the door by my seat. I spent the night in the emergency clinic. They did tests and put a catheter in my urethra. All through the early hours I heard the groans from the other beds, and I was forbidden from drinking any water because they were considering surgery for first thing in the morning.

I fractured the first lumbar vertebra and its left

pedicle. The CAT scan indicated a crack close to the spinal cord, a red speck within a white outline representing the bone and the protection of the motor system from the waist downwards. From the emergency clinic I was transferred to the hospital, and from hospital home a week later. There were fifty days without lifting my head, another three months of physiotherapy and an orthopaedic corset made of polyurethane.

The accident was a kind of drop of water, in a year that began with me going into the CPOR and ended in that bed, with me staring at the ceiling, and deciding to defer college and spend a while abroad was the very least I had to do if I didn't want simply to repeat the whole thing again after my recovery: a course I hated, an internship I didn't want back, the same house and the same city and the same people waiting for me to turn twenty and thirty and forty without having learned anything or forgotten anything at all.

39.

In the first weeks at the CPOR there's a field exercise you do. The whole unit is transported by lorry to Butiá, an hour's drive from Porto Alegre, and you spend the day doing quick dashes, commando crawls and rappelling. You eat rice and bananas. The toilets are chamber pots behind the trees. The day begins before sunrise, in a lake with icy water up to your chest where you do gymnastics with your rifle, and before long you are in a state where you're oblivious to the dirtiness and to the tiredness of marching with your soaked feet headed nowhere.

The exercises took place under the command of Lieutenant Pires. In basic training I was instructed by various different officers, and each one of them was easy to hate: Major Régis, who said ugly women and idiot students get everywhere, like weeds; Captain Juliano, who said I'll shit and piss in the mouth of any student who tries to be smart; and Lieutenant Ricardo, who said the only other place I'd find another platoon like this one would be in a home for spastics. With Pires it was different, first of all because of what he called *spiritual meetings*. He'd wait in Butiá for the arrival of the patrol, a group of eight students who were left out in the bush with a compass and had to find a position at particular coordinates nine kilometres away, a deployment that took all night because you could only move a hundred metres at a time, the point man in front indicating the

vector of the column, thirty degrees north, with additional orientation by the stars if the sky happened to be
clear, and when we arrived we would sit down in a semi-
circle with him standing at the centre and then he would
get his Bible and begin to read from Psalm 12.

40.

Lieutenant Pires liked to say, whoever knows God's
Work will never feel weak, he will never feel defeated.
The lieutenant spoke about the transitory nature of
wealth, about the magnificence of being alive in the
very night of Creation, and before we were dismissed to
sleep and face another eighteen-hour day including a
new patrol and a new selection of passages from the
Bible he would ask each of us, what is your faith, do you
go to worship, does your family fear the Word?

I had never read the Bible before, at least not chron-
ologically and systematically. Up to that point all I knew
about it was the Ten Commandments, Noah's Ark and
other episodes from Genesis that were diluted into the
Afternoon Movie on TV, but in the Butiá training
camp I realised it was worth being a part of Lieutenant
Pires's group: 11 a.m. sitting in the classroom while the

rest of the platoon were doing physical education, twenty-five sprints on the hot tarmac in flimsy plimsolls nicknamed *No-Stars*.

From the Butiá camp onward I came to be what's known in the army as a *peixe*, the teacher's pet, Lieutenant Pires's favourite, because I was able to quote the Old Testament and relate passages to our day-to-day lives in barracks – the exhortation in Deuteronomy to be obedient, the sacrifices of Leviticus, everything that I took out of context in a way that would sound idiotic to anyone who didn't read it literally. One day the lieutenant called me over and said, did you know I was baptised late? I was older than you when I joined the congregation of the Assembleia. The decision changed my life, the lieutenant said, and when the item about Diogo appeared in the daily report I knew that he was to be in charge of the investigation. Diogo would be summoned to explain himself by the end of Friday morning. I might be interrogated, too. I would knock at the door of the officers' mess, I'd ask permission to come in, I'd sit opposite Lieutenant Pires and reply to the only person in the army who liked me – the only person who would be disappointed if I were arrested alongside a student everyone had reasons to despise.

41.

Diogo asked for the equivalent of four monthly salaries not to turn me in. It's so easy to convince yourself
you're right when the person on the other side is a black-
mailer, a worm who crawls around during activities on
the Friday morning before the questioning. The last
shift of the night had ended without incident, the senior
officer coming by on his rounds, then the next column
arriving down the athletics track to relieve me. Despite
Diogo I fell asleep the moment I lay down in my bunk.
Despite having to make a decision about the blackmail,
I slept well and got up rested and ready to do the cleaning. Broom, wax on the banister and black foam: dawn
in the barracks is always a relief, a quiet solidarity
between moving shadows, your nose used to the stench,
the tasks that seem easier because impotence and agony
are put on hold until the next spell of guard duty.

It's so much easier looking at someone like Diogo
and thinking that it wouldn't make any difference
whether he turned me in or not. He was the son of a
police clerk, his grandfather had been a greengrocer,
the grandson becoming a second-grade lieutenant for
eight years after graduating would be the furthest the

family could hope to get. My involvement in the pot episode wouldn't change his expulsion, his four years in some nickel-and-dime college, which he would leave with no job and a student loan he'd never repay, so it would be sensible to try and find a better alternative than succumbing to blackmail.

Psalm 12 says that the impure speak falsely, and the Lord will cut off all flattering lips and the tongue that speaks proud things, but wasn't Lieutenant Pires ready to believe anything I said? Perhaps I ought to warn Diogo: it's up to you whether or not to make this a fight. The guards in the sentry box won't give evidence on your side. They aren't such idiots as to admit that they heard a conversation about pot and didn't report it to the duty officer. And if you want to push me still further, I should perhaps warn Diogo, blameless, with an emphasis that up until that moment had existed only in thought, there's nothing to stop me from saying you were the one to offer the joint.

42.

While I recovered from the accident I would spend my days reading and listening to music. In the late afternoon the corset would be opened and I'd be turned onto my side for my back to be wiped down with a damp cloth. Meals were served on a tray. I learned how to use cutlery staring up at the ceiling. Baths also happened in the late afternoons, then my mother would help to replace the corset, the fit regulated by the velcro strips, and I got used to using bedpans and urinals and not feeling embarrassed as long as I was clean.

There were two doctors looking after me at that time. An orthopaedist, who had taken care of me years earlier when I'd broken my arm, and a spinal expert who assessed whether or not there was any need for surgery. At the moment of impact I felt a compression of my abdomen, and one of the firemen opened the door and said to keep calm, not to move and to try and exhale. He and a colleague pulled me out in a sitting position, my neck and chest were immobilised and he pinched my leg and asked whether I could feel anything.

The accident happened in 1993, and the following year I was in London loading up the basket of sandwiches and working on my feet twelve hours a day. The basket weighed something like ten kilos. I also helped to carry the boxes of provisions for the coffee shop. I kept some casual cleaning jobs, and one time I helped an Indian in Marble Arch to move house, including a sofa and a stone table that it took four people to lift, and from the moment the doctors said that I would be well, that the vertebra would rebuild itself on its own from a fibrocartilage callus, that I wouldn't suffer from neurological or motor after-effects and that only a few months later I'd even be able to run and do sports again, I never stopped thinking about how things would be if the result had been different.

43.

During my time in bed, in London, back in Brazil and even today, I never stopped wondering what would have happened if the impact had been just a little harder: another five kilometres per hour, a few centimetres further forward on the driver's door, or if it hadn't been a fire engine but a VW camper with a refrigerator delivery man who had pulled me out of the scrap metal without any care, the twisted position of the lower back, my body sagging to the left and the rest of the vertebra crushed against the spinal cord.

What words would the doctor say to break the news? What practical measures would be taken in the months after a thing like that? I kept wondering whether there'd have to be some conversion carried out on the house to make the doors wider, the shelves lower, whether a ramp would have to be constructed at the steps leading to the entrance hall, and how long it would be before someone talked to me because decisions needed to be made and then that person would hand me a sample catalogue full of photos – motorised wheelchairs, unmotorised wheelchairs, with hubcaps matt or chrome, with white upholstering on the backrest or pastel-coloured.

44.

How long would it be before I received a visit from my friends, those who knew already and those who would need to be informed by me or by someone else to prepare themselves before coming into the room? The first time when they would see me like this. Pretending it was a visit like any other. What to say about someone in that state at eighteen, how long before you want to distance yourself from that person because the situation is so hard to deal with? How long does it take for half your friends never to visit any more, only a twentieth of them remaining in regular touch, with all the surgeries and the treatments in clinics with exercises for repeating endlessly, waking and having lunch and spending the day with physical pain in a limb that is and isn't there?

A year or two later I would have muscular arms, a swollen face, a urine bag and with any luck the ability to go into the bathroom and clean myself all on my own, something I would do two or three times a day and each time I'd be grateful that the humiliation wasn't even worse, and if I were lucky enough to go to bed with a woman on top or in some position that would need to be explained and rehearsed I would also remember that perhaps she is only there out of curiosity, or pity, and I'd try to see this in her face, too, the grimace of pain or effort that would make it clear that I would never be the same again, and nobody's life has stopped because of me, and nobody is guilty of anything, and how long before I decide whether or not that is worth facing?

45.

Another possible difference between Immaculée and Kurt Cobain: she buried her family, left Rwanda, married in the United States, had two children, wrote a book and travelled the world knowing she would never be asked to speak on any other subject than the ninety-one days she spent in the bathroom, and even so she returned to Africa and visited the man who killed her father, her mother and her brother, and put her hand on his shoulder, and between giving his guilt some relief and abandoning him to a still darker horror she chose to forgive him.

Whereas Kurt Cobain wrote his letter, walked across the greenhouse, sat down on two towels on the terrace, took his hunting cap, smoked a cigarette, another gulp of beer, another hit of black Mexican heroin just above the elbow, the last thing left to do before holding the barrel of the rifle to the roof of his mouth, and I don't know whether at any of these moments he wondered what the next day would be like for Courtney Love. I don't know if he remembered that her band's album was due to be released that week. And that forever after people would say that she made her husband get addicted, that she didn't support him during detox, that she was ready to abandon him in the worst situation a human being can find themselves, and how without her everything might have turned out differently.

46.

I keep wondering what Courtney Love must have thought when she read those reports. When she heard the speculations about there being none of Kurt Cobain's fingerprints on the gun, or that the handwriting on the goodbye note wasn't his, or that her husband's estate with the addition of future earnings was in the region of tens of millions of dollars. I keep wondering if she saw the documentary by a film-maker who accuses her almost formally of murder. If hours after the death she already knew that she would become a part of the legend, and that for the rest of her life she would no longer be the daughter of the Grateful Dead's first manager, or the girl from San Francisco who studied in Europe, or the singer from Hole, or the actress in two Miloš Forman movies, or anything other than the person who was linked to an inexplicable act that everybody believed they could explain.

47.

I imagine Frances Bean reading the articles years later, the things they said about her father, the things they said about her mother and about herself. I imagine her at school. At a party where they start playing a Nirvana song. At a coffee shop with her friends and someone approaches and asks shyly, are you really who I think you are? And another person approaches shyly and asks if she knew about the battles over her custody, the Los Angeles Department of Child Services, Kurt Cobain declaring in an interview that he was terrified of his daughter's life ending up like his own.

I wonder whether when he fired the shot Kurt Cobain didn't know this, if he'd never heard about what happens to the children of someone who does what he did, especially small children who would never get the chance to talk to their father, hear his reasons, believe in them or not depending on the arguments he makes, his tone of voice, his look, the environment in which this is said and which helps to evaluate his sincerity, a father denying the questions that any child asks herself when she is included in such a story without ever having asked to be: whether the life he found so unbearable wasn't the life he'd started to have after her birth and because of it.

48.

Valéria was four years old when her mother died in a car crash. One's earliest memory of a person can be an image, a sound. For Valéria it's a pink room, a mobile hanging by the bed, her mother or her own dream of her mother holding a book and a lullaby which for a long time her father still continued to put on the electric turntable. She didn't go to the funeral, and if she had gone she wouldn't have remembered it. She didn't keep a toy, and if she had kept one she wouldn't have been able to say when her mother had bought it. She never read that book again, nor heard that record, and she quickly grew out of the clothes, and she and her father moved out of the apartment less than two years later.

The death took place on a night that Valéria attempted to reconstruct. How often she went down that stretch of Salvador França, with that deviation, not quite a curve, the tarmac and the hard shoulder and a tree that's still there today, the position of the trunk and the grass that grew back and is no different from the part that never got torn up. Valéria spent years trying to understand what her mother was doing on Salvador França, where she was going, whether she was aware of the moment when the speed and friction meant there was no other possibility than to crash head-on at a time when people didn't use seat belts and the Beetle's engine and the greatest resistance of its bodywork were at the back.

For a long time Valéria used to look up at the sky and quietly speak her mother's name. At bedtime she would close her eyes, and it was as though the name were a presence. On her first birthday after the accident she waited till the very end because she was sure her mother would come. She didn't remember or didn't know whether her mother was good-tempered. She didn't remember or didn't know whether her mother liked children. She didn't remember or didn't know whether her mother was also in the habit of crying in the dark. But she remembered and knew, because her father told her, on one of the few occasions when he felt willing to share details of the only woman he ever married, that she had her mother's voice.

49.

I don't know whether in the middle of one of our band practices Valéria ever stopped to think that she was only there because something had survived that night on Salvador França: her taste in music, her way of singing and a characteristic that might be talent or fate. At the age of seven her father gave her an album by Black Sabbath. Drawing a line from the bands of the 1970s to what was being listened to in 1993 there's as much connection between Nirvana and the punk movement, if you consider the speed and simplicity of the arrangements, the attitude and rejection of success that were inherited by the university and indie circuit, as there is with the first heavy metal – the melody, the dynamics, the romanticism with no trace of the irony or the boredom or the sense of spectacle of the 1980s mainstream.

There are several different definitions of romanticism, and a good proportion of them include notions of purity and conviction, the yearning for an ideal that transcends the banality or distortion of the time in which one lives, which can easily drain out into rebellion and madness. The poster of Kurt Cobain in Valéria's house was a well-known photo, him standing in front of a sign saying *Believe on the Lord Jesus Christ and Thou Shalt Be Saved,* and the possible sarcasm in the set-up is only there for those who don't know the singer's biography: the visits to church in his boyhood, his interest in the Jain idea of heaven and hell, his discourse of lamentation when faced with the corruption of the world, his speaking out against violence, sexism and homophobia that were a kind of belief disguised beneath a cloak of nihilism and unpretension. I don't know what most attracted Valéria to him, whether it was the sound that needed no justifying, the barrage of pop noise that could have made Nirvana a stadium group like any other, or the premature embodiment of the myth, itself also romantic, that would be consolidated in April 1994.

50.

The first gig with Valéria on vocals took place six months before Hollywood Rock. I was on the left side of the stage, on a night when several bands played one after another to thirty stoners in a place with puddles on the floor and a faulty sound desk. I didn't turn my guitar towards the amplifier because of the microphonics, I didn't test the pedals before playing my first chords, six quick numbers and the delayed feedback in a uniform clump of distortion, and even then in the first row and the second nobody could take their eyes off her.

Writing music on the electric guitar isn't hard. You can combine chords over- or under-tuned or use pedals so that a C doesn't sound quite like a C, but in general the bass line is simple and the lyrics are done in ten minutes with the odd amendment during practice. The lyrics I wrote weren't very different from those by any other eighteen-year-old songwriter, with the basic theme of feeling something you can't express and which may or not have political or amorous or existential resonances, but what does make the difference between playing to those thirty stoners or being awarded three platinum discs like Kurt Cobain is the way the whole thing is said, the luck and the personal history of the person saying it, their nationality, class, appearance, clothing and atti- tude. Their talent, which is as arbitrary as being born blond or dark-skinned, with a voice that can or can't reach a particular pitch, or a particular timbre or depth, or a particular degree of intensity that suggests the exist- ence of something dark and beautiful inside you.

Valéria used to like asking what I would do if I

learned that she was sick. Not a sickness that was easy to feel solidarity for, like arthritis or a heart condition that might never manifest itself, but a debilitating ailment that required commitment for a future that was certain – with her depending on me to take a bath or to change her nappies because of, say, multiple sclerosis, Parkinson's, cancer. She used to ask: can you see me beyond the beauty? Can you imagine what it'll be like when I'm old? I'll never know whether the impression she conveyed when she held the microphone was or wasn't connected to this behaviour, which was most distinctive in Valéria, and of all the things I lived through in those eleven months none was more striking than my doubts about what she really meant: and what if tomorrow I'm in an accident and I'm disfigured? And what if my body becomes repellent? And what if I start to smell bad, to rot away before your very eyes? Can anybody say that they love another person if they don't take this test?

51.

Growing up reading about music is like self-help in reverse. Valéria knew the fate of each one of those heroes, Jim Morrison drowned in a bathtub, Jimi Hendrix's body in a hotel bed, the washing line that hanged Ian Curtis, Sid Vicious and the suicide pact with Nancy Spungen. With the hindsight of fate it wouldn't be hard to make a connection between her idealised images and the way she started to behave from the first gig, her expectations concerning me, the questions that began to have a meaning that was no longer the obvious meaning, though at first I thought it was all no more than a running joke. Valéria made me swear that I would take care of her. That I would never hurt her. That I wouldn't leave, not even if she had a sudden psychotic attack, if she spent the rest of her days in a hospice.

What happens when you can't see beyond the beauty? The expression on Valéria's face when she said these things may have seemed ironic or charming because I was hypnotised by her, and so I would laugh and she would laugh back and it didn't matter that she made me describe my visits to the hospice, the days and the schedules, what the screening process at the entrance was like and how I was dressed and whether I brought presents and if I still liked her when the medicines had left her light-headed and bloated, unable to follow the conversation, and how one day when I arrive they inform me that she has been transferred to a different sector because of an episode involving a pair of scissors and an entire floor that was almost destroyed by fire.

On the night we met Valéria said, be careful there's a chance I might like it, and if I do are you ready to go all the way? To say goodbye to what your life has been up till now? Are you ready to surrender everything you have? she asked with her white teeth, her eyes that were greenish in the light, her upper lip, her lower lip, her nose, her chin, her neck, her arms, her waist, her legs, and with the hindsight of fate I can only mourn how little of these conversations it is possible to reconstruct, a description of the setting, the objective facts and dates, because the feeling of being trapped by the power of her physical presence is something which today seems incomprehensible, like when you talk about yourself as a baby and can only understand that baby by looking at it from the outside, using the tools of someone who is older, in practice another person, because it is not possible to go back to being naïve once you have stopped being so.

52.

It may be that I was still naïve at the time of our band's first gig. There were women in the audience, a few of them dancing a couple of metres from the stage, and it was a novelty to have them looking at me, too, after so many years of being rejected because of my clothes, my age, my hair, what I said or didn't say, what I did or failed to do on so many nights when I left home knowing I'd be ignored or despised, and it's a shock because all you have to do is put in a plug and play a three-chord riff and stay standing up for forty minutes on a stage for the world to turn itself inside out.

I don't know whether Valéria also noticed the change, or whether it was natural to her that I should be sought out after the gig, and praised for playing well, and that this just became so frequent that she began to be bothered by it. Once she kicked off because the waitress had apparently smiled at me. That night she drank more than usual. I tried to ignore the accusations, she got even more pointed, I lost patience and said excuse me and left the restaurant, and two hours later the entryphone rings and Valéria is reeling and yelling at all the neighbours, where the hell do you get the nerve to do this to me?

With Valéria I learned to end an argument out of sheer tiredness: four in the morning and I'd take her home and put her to bed unconscious and lie there in the dark for some time before closing my eyes. I also learned that things would calm down with a few days' distance, during which time I'd argue to myself as though she were listening and agreeing with all my points of view. I also learned that none of these hypothetical arguments I made would ever be understood, because it wasn't a question of logic, a debate to be won in a considered, rational fashion, making use of the resources of intelligence and language, but rather relative to the question: why should I put myself through all this?

53.

A question that was also this: why am I unable to act differently? Ever since the beginning of our relationship that had been the way things worked, and it's easy to repeat the same pattern night after night when the air is cool on the way out of the show, and there's one night when Valéria leaves earlier saying I was never to come see her again, and it's the second time she's done it this week alone, and on the way out there's a taxi and someone inside asks if I want a lift. On that night Valéria is not keeping watch, she isn't hiding behind a tree as if to confirm the accusations she's now in the habit of making: the way I behave with a female friend, the way I look at a girl who's handing out promo flyers at a traffic light; and so I get into the taxi and sit in the back seat and the girl says her name's Tati and she slides towards me.

54.

I accept a lift from Tati, but I turn down the move she makes. I turn down other advances from her, once on the phone, once at a bar where she appears to have followed me, till one day I'm at a party and I go into a bathroom which someone has forgotten to lock, and Tati's there snorting coke and she says what a pleasant surprise, make yourself comfortable, and I drop my trousers and while she leans over the sink I'm looking at myself in the mirror, the man on the guitar, to the left of the stage, and though Valéria's at the same party I don't wonder whether anyone saw me opening the door and taking such a long time to come out again.

The hindsight of fate tells me I might have been able to predict the sequence that came next, because Valéria had had relationships before and I should perhaps have known something about them, how they began and how they ended, the views of her ex-boyfriends, what they would be able to tell me if I put out an appeal saying that knowing about her past was essential if I were not to fall into the trap. If I'd known, I could have been more careful, because I didn't have the least experience of dissembling, nor the slightest skill at lying aged eighteen, and it was only a matter of time before I betrayed myself out of stupidity or nerves or guilt at the party where Valéria knocked on the bathroom door and knocked again until I opened it and there was nothing more to be said.

If at the time I had met any of Valéria's ex-boyfriends, I could have been alerted to the ramifications of that scene: me at the bathroom door, Tati behind me, and then Valéria looks at me and at Tati and when I think something is about to be said she turns her back and leaves the party. I don't see her again until a week later. My going to her apartment. The two of us sitting on the bed. It's the first time I've said sorry for something like this, an eighteen-year-old's customs of guilt and humility, and how am I to assess the way Valéria will take this apology? What does she think of the person in front of her as he describes the details of what happened in the bathroom?

55.

At eighteen you can't imagine that this is the real trap. That there might be something else behind what appears to be generosity, the first girlfriend who says tell me the truth, be honest with me because I'll be able to tell otherwise, it's easier for me to forgive you if I know what it was like. And so I tell her about the open door, the sink counter, Tati's face looking in the mirror. Valéria asks if I liked it, if I'd do it again, and I talk and she listens and it even seems that things have been resolved until I get to know her for real.

56.

Nowadays there is an ambiguity in the way we deal with the issue of illness. Even as we talk about the advantages of a healthy life, which includes food, physical exercise, a limit on tobacco, and an aesthetic and behavioural pattern hammered into us through advertising and television and government campaigns, there's simultaneously a kind of glamour surrounding neuroses. It's hard to find a Hollywood movie whose hero demonstrates conventional patterns of behaviour. There's nothing more popular on social networks than to appear discontented, excessive, unpredictable, a modest version of the cliché that sees genius as an extension of madness. When Kurt Cobain died, there wasn't an obituary that failed to make the connection between his suicide and a kind of artistic, sensitive soul, defenceless against a world that was neither artistic nor sensitive, which made him *lacerate himself until he found a vocabulary within himself that was capable of saying what he really meant*. Nobody would actually have published such a piece, and that example was only one of dozens, written by solitary types who eat frozen meals in one-bedroom apartments and like showing the public how much they know about the hard life of celebrities, if the death in question had been the result of a heart attack or appendicitis, a stroke or toxoplasmosis. No musical icon reaches a peak of popularity and interest quite like one who knowingly seeks out his own end. No romantic relationship seems real without its dose of intensity, chaos and mutual destruction, and to this day I ask myself what, faced with the choice, I would have chosen – physical illness or mental illness, each of the same severity and arising at the same time, their consequences visible and invisible for the remainder of my years, whether I were choosing for Valéria or for myself.

57.

Valéria had a few boyfriends before me, but only one who was serious. His name was Alexandre, and if I'd met him in the days of the Independência bar, the thing I only discovered after the incident with Tati wouldn't have come as a surprise, or, if it did, as the confirmation of merely a vague suspicion. Less than a week after I confessed everything we were in a bar, where Valéria spoke up close with all the men there, sometimes laying a hand on their arms, and from then on she never missed a chance to mention that she'd had someone making a pass at her on the bus, in a clothing store, in the middle of the road.

With the hindsight of fate I couldn't say which came first, Valéria's behaviour or the way her questions began to sound different, the way she wanted to know whether it's possible to avoid being tested in this way. Whether it's possible to like someone without knowing the worst of them, without being hurt by the other person, destroyed along with him, and I didn't understand what she meant until she began to tell more stories about how she'd accepted somebody's invitation to go for a beer, what that person's house was like afterwards, and how that person sat down next to her on the sofa, poured a bit more to drink, and then her stories always stopped halfway through because she wanted me to ask what had happened in the end and I never asked and the following week she'd be back with a plot-line that went a little bit further, the two of them have got up off the sofa, the hallway, the bedroom, a bedside lamp, and I didn't know whether or not the story was true and I tried not to think about it until Nail showed up as a character.

The only thing I kept from Valéria was a postcard sent from São Paulo. It's a photo of the Chá viaduct, on the back it has my name and address and it was stamped by the post office where she had taken it on the Friday.

Regular post would have taken three or four working days to reach Porto Alegre: I would have received the card on Wednesday or Thursday following, after the doorman left it in our doorway, risking someone else reading it before me, my father, my mother. But Valéria didn't want to trust to the regular post to get my eventual reaction. Why did she imagine we wouldn't be seeing each other before I read her message? That I wouldn't change my mind and go to São Paulo that Friday? That I wouldn't figure out some way of getting rid of Diogo, of the lieutenant, prison, army, of Porto Alegre and everything that conspired for Nail to be alone with her at the moment when Kurt Cobain stepped onto the stage?

58.

Valéria's mother died when she was four years old. In the only conversation she had about it with her father, he told her there had been a row that night, another one of those arguments Valéria didn't remember witnessing, with pieces of information she then used to assemble in order to set the scene the way she wanted it, her mother grabbing the car keys and her father trying to stop her because it was raining and she seemed more than usually on edge.

For a long time Valéria forced herself not to think of anything before going to sleep. It wasn't easy because the outlines of an armchair and the curtains lit by the slits in a venetian blind looked like the bonnet of a car, and all she could hear were the words of an aunt who visited her father after the burial, who while her father went to the kitchen to fetch a jug of juice remarked to her husband that in the accident Valéria's mother had been ripped in two. *Ripped in two*, and then you close your eyes and the car bonnet is still there, the noise, the fire, her mother's arm yanked out the way you yank a doll who has been trodden on again and again.

Some nights never end when you think about what leads someone to drive so quickly in the rain, legs crushed and the person herself between pieces of metal, and the flames are the last thing the person sees before everything goes dark. Valéria was never able to say whether her anger at her mother was mere selfishness, whether she had the right to want her mother to be alive despite what her father told her in that one conversation, about the depression and the medicines and two previous threats to do something stupid, her father hearing the car tyres two floors below shortly after she slammed the apartment door on that rainy night; or whether it was disappointment that her mother hadn't thought of her during her journey to Salvador França, how many traffic lights she would have waited at, how many curves or straight stretches of road where she could have remembered Valéria sleeping or going to the bedroom door to peek at her father and see what was going on after so much noise, four years old and Valéria is unable to say anything about that night because everything is blocked out by the repeating questions, why did her mother make this decision, why didn't she step on the brake, why did she decide to accelerate towards the tree and leave me here alone.

59.

It takes a certain amount of courage to hurt oneself on purpose. Some people spend their whole lives unable to give themselves an injection. Not just anybody can get a splinter out using the tip of a penknife. It's easier to think of taking a whole bottle of medicine and sleeping forever without feeling anything more, than to slam a door on your own index finger. In the abstract it's possible to decide to take some action, a bullet tearing through flesh, a rope squeezing a neck, a stomach burning from the poison, bones crushed after jumping out the window. The problem is when you're lying in a bed after an accident with a fire engine and you spend much of the day thinking about what it would be like to go all the way. Which method would be quickest, surest. How many days after learning the news about the wheelchair. Would it make a difference waiting a week, during which time I'd do what exactly? Eat something I fancied? Write a note like Kurt Cobain?

60.

I wonder if it's normal to think this kind of thing when you're more than eighteen years old? Kurt Cobain was twenty-seven in April of 1994. Immaculée Ilibagiza, twenty-two. I don't know if it's something a person is born with, a defective gene that from time to time makes the brain turn against itself, or if it's a place anyone might be able to reach through environmental factors, so that a simple romantic disappointment or the example set by an idol or a person close to you makes you contradict the species' natural instinct. In any case, it's more common to imagine yourself going through with it when you're younger. As the years go by this kind of reasoning starts to seem like nonsense, a symptom of someone who has not yet truly lived, who has not learned to suffer and to fall and to start over again, something that happens every day and to everyone. Up till that point there's always the comfort of imagining that it depends on you alone.

61.

On the morning I got back on my feet my mother came into the bedroom shortly before lunch. She had gone to the doctor, he showed her the second X-ray of the vertebra and said I could walk straight away. It was as though I hadn't been immobile for fifty days: raise the torso first, just my head for a few minutes so as not to get dizzy, then a while sitting down with my legs outside the bed. I remember I was astonished at my memory of the movements, a body obeying commands without hesitation, the mechanics and balance so easy for someone lucky enough to have had a lesion in the bone next to the spinal cord that was two millimetres smaller than it might have been.

Lieutenant Pires came to visit me during my recovery. Before talking to me he asked my mother if I was eating properly, sleeping, in a good mood. The important thing is to keep your head in good shape, he said, and when we were alone he handed me a Bible with several pages marked in it. Ecclesiastes 1:18, he who increases knowledge increases sorrow. I Chronicles 22:14, in my affliction I have prepared a hundred thousand talents of gold. It was the first time we'd spoken about religion since I'd stopped attending the eleven o'clock group. I know you're resisting, he said, but now's the moment to think about this. I'm not giving you any advice, just try to read a passage or two before going to sleep.

62.

The last time I attended the eleven o'clock group was the morning after the first shift on guard, when I still hadn't made my decision. Diogo would soon be called to testify, and I was still hesitating. Not only because surely the lieutenant wasn't really so stupid, even he might realise Diogo had no reason to lie and nobody makes up a story like that from scratch. Not only because Diogo would spend thirty days locked up, saying that I had lied, and there was nothing to stop him saying I'd squealed to the fat sergeant, and the rest of the year I'd be hated by every one of the two hundred students in a place where that's the worst possible thing that can happen. Not only because Diogo had nothing to lose, and all I needed to do was mention the possibility of challenging him for him to launch himself at me, and I'd defend myself, and whatever else happened we'd both be detained for fighting before either of us was able to explain who'd provoked whom.

The gathering of the spiritual group ended at midday, after another half-dozen proverbs and symbolic passages that Lieutenant Pires was able to interpret only literally, and my hesitation was not just about what would happen if I got up and chanced not to run into Diogo, and if there was time for me to get my rucksack and put on my out-of-barracks uniform and present myself at the gate with the entire barracks. What would happen if I passed by the sentry box, at the normal time on a Friday half-day? What would happen if I went home and got my things and was at the airport before four o'clock to bring my ticket forward? It depended on me alone, and on Monday I'd be back and I would or would not face the consequences of having left, a gesture which technically wasn't running away, at a time when there weren't cellphones and it was reasonable for me to travel on a weekend because I had not been notified that I was implicated in a disciplinary inquiry.

63.

My hesitation wasn't to do with any of this, but with Valéria. When the band's first gig had come to an end, the owner of the bar asked us if we fancied another the following week. Then he wanted us to play at a friend's club in São Leopoldo. We began to be scheduled for one gig after another, and I was sure that there was only one reason for this, the 'singing revelation' as one producer put it, the guy who offered us a tour round Serra and then Cachoeira and Passa Fundo and, who knows, maybe a record with the label he claimed to represent.

I didn't tell anyone in the CPOR that I had a band. In those days it was expensive to record a simple promo track, and it wasn't common to give interviews or to produce a video so soon into a career. It's unlikely that any of the students would have been at any of our performances and recognised me. In any case, my going into the barracks complicated any plans to travel or to rent a studio, or to invest in something that might or not transform everybody's future even if I did also manage to maintain a peaceful relationship with Valéria.

After the incident with Tati, Valéria began to accuse me of only being with her because of the band. It's really so convenient for you, she said: you just have to pretend to be interested. You just have to lie to me and I'll do whatever you say. Want a nice song? Want me to dance, too? Then you introduce me like I'm your pet. And you look at every woman who walks by. And invite every one of them for a private little meeting, isn't that right? Then you lock the bathroom door. How do you do it, you just open your flies and tell them to kneel down? You don't even say please? Not even a thank-you afterwards?

64.

The first meeting with the record producer took place in his office. In truth, it was a stockroom at the back of a hardware store, a place filled with assorted coils of things, with a formica table and a thermos of past-its-best coffee, and of course it wasn't long before Valéria was telling me that the producer had invited her for a beer, just the two of them. And he'd pressed his leg up against hers before the conversation had even begun. And she'd moved her leg away, and he'd pressed up against her again, and it was this little story that finally made me react.

It happened at a practice session ten days before the Nirvana show. It was one of the few times in 1993 the band had got together, because by the first week of January I was already at the CPOR and it took a while for me to find the time and inclination in a period when all I wanted to do was sleep. As I slept I forgot about Kurt Cobain, about Lieutenant Pires, about the rows with Valéria and the doubts I'd always had, even before the incident with Tati, and actually I could say that the incident with Tati had been a reaction to my doubts, that there was no way I hadn't seen it coming from the very beginning, as I listened in silence, witnessing my first girlfriend's theatrics ever since the day I introduced her to Nail.

65.

Right from the start of our relationship I noticed how Nail behaved towards Valéria. Soon somebody mentioned they'd seen the two of them at a party. One time she was sitting between me and him and there was a moment when she took his hand and he didn't pull it away, and that lasted a second longer than necessary, or a fraction of a second, and Valéria's stories of people making a pass at her got all mixed up with my suspicion and she must have noticed because she then started making a point of mentioning his name.

I never said to Valéria that the incident with Tati was a kind of reply. That when I joined Tati in the bathroom it was Valéria and Nail I was thinking about, because if she could do it to me then I could also do it to her. It's so painful to be aware that you're trapped as I was, hypnotised by Valéria and Valéria taking advantage of this, tired of being in her hands and feeling humiliated each time she mentioned how sensitive Nail was, how devoted, how talented.

I never saw Tati again after getting caught with her in the bathroom. I didn't even finish what I was meant to have done with her, because I'd been drinking and the bathroom was a squeeze and my face in the mirror started looking weird in the white light, slightly deformed, slightly sad, and you only have to notice this for excitement to give way to something like horror, and you apologise and pull up your trousers and when you're just about to go without even washing your hands you hear Valéria yelling and banging on the door.

66.

The practice session when I finally reacted began with Valeria testing me. She spent the whole time looking at Nail, and sang all the songs turned towards him. It was a hot evening, she'd drunk a bottle of white wine and she started to ask him about the producer. What would he do if his girlfriend had someone making a pass at her? Would he keep on meeting the producer? Would you exchange your girlfriend for a tour? How much does it cost to make a record? Would you say that's a good price for someone like me?

I would guess that Alexandre, Valéria's first real boyfriend, had girlfriends after her. And that he was dumped by some of them. And that he dumped some of them, too. And these girls had also had boyfriends, and had dumped and been dumped by them, and the sum total of so many dumpings will have created some kind of protocol based on experience. I would guess that things become progressively less serious, even if only on account of the statistics, and with every ten or twenty or fifty outcomes the chances of one turning out like the one with Alexandre and Valéria decreases because it's only normal that you'd try to avoid putting yourself through such a thing repeatedly.

If I had spoken to Alexandre as soon as I met Valéria, the outcome might perhaps have been different. And at band practice I wouldn't have thought about Nail, about the producer, about the veracity or otherwise of Valéria's stories, the final drop of water after weeks of restraining myself so as not to give in to an impulse that had nothing to do with the future of the band: the microphone was on, Valéria was continuing to provoke me, I turned my back and when I was opening the door to leave I heard the crash, a kick at the stand and the wine bottle shattering against the wall close to me, and I said what the hell was that and Nail said take it easy and Valéria said fuck taking it easy, and I walked over and Nail stepped into my way and I threw a punch which didn't quite connect with him, and then another punch that got him in the ear, and a third, and when I sat down on the pavement outside the studio my blood pressure dropped and everyone had left and I was so angry I thought I was going to throw up.

67.

If I'd talked to Alexandre beforehand, maybe I could have predicted Valéria's reaction to our fight. What it would mean to her for me to be sitting on the pavement after practice, then lying down, legs bent to get my blood flowing again and me getting up and walking home knowing that something had changed forever. A band can end in lots of ways and for lots of reasons, and even if there was no way of going back at that point, the record we never made, the gigs we never played, the producer I never heard from again, the memory that was lost with those who knew me in the Porto Alegre of two decades ago – even if the fate of the band had been sealed with that argument, things with Valéria could still have been different.

Perhaps Valéria had been waiting for that fight. Perhaps it was what she'd been asking of me for weeks, ever since the incident with Tati, the prolonged interval between my shamed declaration of repentance and the punches I threw at Nail. Or perhaps more was needed, and I ought to run away from the barracks on Friday as a second proof, accepting that I would be arrested on my return because the four monthly salaries for

silencing Diogo were the money I'd spent on my bus
ticket, on the ticket for the Nirvana show, and what I'd
put aside for transport, food and other expenses in São
Paulo. But perhaps the cycle would not be concluded in
the second conversation I had with Valéria either, after
the final practice, our last meeting before she went off
to São Paulo, and the question she asked this time without any anger, without any hurt, without any intention
of revenge like she'd had in the previous conversation
about Tati.

Valéria asked if I really did want to stay together,
and in all the relationships I had later I thought about
this answer: whether it's possible not to confuse the suffering of being separated from someone, the sadness
because you'll never see this person again, the feeling
of loneliness after three days, a month, twenty years,
with the only thing that ought to count in such cases. I
don't know if anyone ever forgets the first time that happens. Or the first time you realise that a single gesture
is enough to make the outcome inevitable, a word in a
conversation just a few minutes long that brings everything you know about the person together into your
memory: Valéria's appearance will always be as in that
conversation, Valeria in a T-shirt and earrings, her

perfume when she hugged me after saying the punches didn't matter, the argument, my attitude over the previous weeks, or what she had done or not done for the situation to have reached that point, and she said sorry and that she understood I was sorry, too, and that if I didn't go to São Paulo it was only because I didn't want to, cos I was too proud, cos I was too much of a coward to admit I wanted the same as her, and I only had to say the word and she'd tell Nail to go to hell and she'd travel with me and we'd start again now, for real.

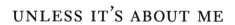

UNLESS IT'S ABOUT ME

68.

When Lieutenant Pires showed up at the hospital, the results from the MRI and the CAT scan had already come in. Since he knew I was going to get well, his tone as he told me he had been converted two years prior to entering the Agulhas Negras Military Academy was not one of compassion or awkwardness. His baptism took place in a brook. A bespectacled pastor dressed in white said that Jesus would come down from the clouds in all his power and glory, and the lieutenant answered amen. The pastor made the lieutenant go under, on his back, and he said it is the law written on your heart, if narrow is the way then strait too is the gate, accept the purity of the waters and when you reach the end of the journey you shall be in heaven.

69.

The lieutenant was twenty-seven years old in 1993. He was married and he had a son who was learning to talk. Before meeting his wife, he had been ready to give up on his studies. When he was fifteen his father had found him drinking beer in a bar close to where the two of them lived, in a suburb of Vitória. The bar had a snooker table and a blind man who collected up the bets. The lieutenant's father beat him with his belt and the broom handle, no son of mine is going to turn into a druggy or a drunk, and he's not becoming a thief and he's not going with whores, and after ten days' punishment the son was sent to live in the house of a relative up in Bahia.

From sixteen to eighteen, without his father close by, not knowing what he was going to do with his life, the lieutenant almost lost himself because of The Bottle. He would have ended up as a tramp if he had not sought out Succour. Numbers 6:3, Hosea 4:11, and the lieutenant explained that sometimes you need to recognise the signs: if he hadn't met his wife, he never would have found The Way. He never would have returned to his studies. His wife attended the Church of the Plenitude of the Throne of God and assured him that he would spend his time cared for, fed, and filled with the moral strength he needed to face up to the Academia exams, and the four years he spent in Resende learning to say yes sir with his backbone very straight because that's what teaches you to be a good commander, were not wasted in indolence and vice.

The lieutenant came to the hospital to talk about the inquiry that had been opened into the firemen. Customary practice dictates that the officer responsible for the platoon of the student injured in an accident should be notified of the details. The man who had been driving the fire engine described the moment I went through the traffic light, the position of the car and the way I was pulled out and taken away in the ambulance. Nobody was hurt apart from me. There was no failure of care. The insurance would pay for the damage to the car and the fire engine, and I confirmed the version of events that said I was drunk at the moment of the collision.

70.

I've been drinking and driving ever since I got my licence. In Porto Alegre it was quite common to do the circuit round 24 Outubro Avenue, around Independência, Osvaldo Aranha, downtown and the Zona Sul, popping into a bar at each stop. It was quite common to go to some neighbouring city, Canoas or Novo Hamburgo, and take the highway back home after having thrown up and fallen asleep on some step or in some gutter. One time I went to Caxias, to a wedding that ended at about five in the morning, and came back alone having mixed champagne, whiskey and cocaine.

There's a whole safety procedure for when you drive drunk. You slow down and flash your high-beams at every junction, even when the lights are in your favour, and you remain aware that the naturalness of each manoeuvre is slightly off what is instinctive, so the speed will seem slow, the amount of space more than ample, the sound of the tape player at too high a volume, the cars and pedestrians too far away, but of course this is no kind of defence. Of course there are scientific experiments on altered reflexes. In hospital I talked to the lieutenant knowing that he knew about the caipirinhas I'd drunk that night, and I had already seen a vast number of news reports about accidents, the Department of Transit campaigns, the stories of victims' families, of people who for ever after had to take care of an invalid, somebody who just happened to be on a pedestrian crossing when some irresponsible driver came along, and I knew the lieutenant knew that running the risk of destroying my life and the lives of other people had still been a choice.

71.

Is that how it works? I spent my whole time in the barracks doing tasks I didn't want to do, being ordered around by people I despised, in the interest of some goals that made no sense at all, a regime of slavery that was established gratuitously, and did I at any point on night duty with three two-hour shifts, standing guard alone in the dark, ever look at the rifle and think it would all be so easy and so quick, a magazine with six bullets at my disposal, each one of them able to propel the brains of a grown man metres away?

In law there's such a thing as aggravated manslaughter, the act of consciously taking on the risk of committing a crime by means of behaviour involving imprudence, negligence or malpractice. That's the case with someone who drives drunk, and I keep thinking about whether the driver doesn't also make a kind of pact at the moment of the first caipirinha or whether he just thinks about the lime and the sugar and the feeling of lightness and then euphoria so rare in a year when everything's gone wrong from the start. Two decades later, when memories are all muddled up with the awareness of what then happened, the guilt and the relief at it all being merely a chapter of the past, the futility of having wanted to be part of a heroic plotline of survival which might include drugs or dangerous sports or journeys to wildernesses where you might find a wild animal or a psychopath, or a mugging that might happen to you or the potential illnesses when you smoke or eat fat or screw without a condom – could I really assure you this was what I was thinking about or this was what I intended or this was the possibility that was on my horizon when I ordered my second caipirinha and my third and my fourth and my fifth and my sixth?

In the twenty years that followed 1993 I eventually came to hate my jobs, the relationships that didn't work out, and I also felt sad and exhausted, ill and defeated, and I could list ten or twenty or ninety situations in which it's tempting to think everything was over too soon, and as such there is no more pain and no more problems and we're merely fulfilling the final acts of a farce controlled by a puppeteer who likes to play. It's true that not everyone's born with the defective gene that allows them to get beyond that daydreaming moment, so eventually you end the work day or the relationship or whatever you need to, a person like any other, thinking how good it is to go for a walk after the rain and smell the grass and have some soup and sleep nice and warm under a blanket on your birthday, but the fact is that moment does exist. It can decide the course for someone born destined to face it, and that's why in forty years of a well-analysed life the only time that remains in a shadow zone is the period around the show by Nirvana.

72.

The note Kurt Cobain left was written in red ink, it was addressed to an imaginary friend from his child-hood and ended with a quote from Neil Young: it's better to burn out than to fade away. The Brazilian edition of the memoirs of Immaculée Ilibagiza has a grey jacket and a photo of her with a bird in the background, and the penultimate line of its more than three hundred pages is: I believe that we can heal Rwanda – and our world – by healing one heart at a time.

Is the fact that Kurt Cobain became so influential and well respected, despite his indifference, that he mentions his daughter's future sadness without considering that its cause will be the same that provoked that letter, while Immaculée's voice is heard only by nuns and goody-two-shoes students like the ones who were at the PUC lecture, despite the generosity of what she has to offer, due entirely to his status as a musical celebrity? And if Immaculée had been the suicide and the tenor of their words had been reversed, with her appealing to a romantic cause to disguise her own giving-up, and Kurt Cobain preaching solidarity through a piece of prose closely resembling self-help, might the story have been different?

What do the appearance, syntax and style of a text tell you about the person who wrote it? The postcard I received from Valéria had a white background, little handwriting in ballpoint pen and just a quote from

'Drain You': eight short lines in a slight misquotation, a cadence that sounds somehow wrong, and whenever someone talks about the message behind Kurt Cobain's lyrics all I want to do is ask whether this person honestly understands what they're really saying, whether they have the first clue about the context in which that thing was written, the incidents and references and in-jokes that connect fragments that are themselves barely above the commonplace, a logorrhoea of banalities that will gain greater meaning only because they are accompanied by the direct emotional appeal that comes from the music, a famous singer and addict from Aberdeen who would have been no more than a famous singer and addict from Aberdeen if in 1993 his story had not been linked to somebody in Porto Alegre who misunderstood the whole thing.

73.

There are figures in the Bible who committed suicide: Abimelech, Saul, Ahithophel, Zimri, Judas, possibly Samson. Lieutenant Pires was better acquainted with the New Testament than the Old, and even that wasn't much for someone who spent years dedicated to

a single book, so when he paid his visit to the hospital I
was the one who was able to say something on the matter: the most modern interpretation of the Gospel, the
sin of tearing oneself away from the greatest of gifts, in
conflict with the guarantee of eternal life we receive
when we accept Christ. I could continue to use language that would distract the lieutenant, the phrases I'd
learned in the previous months, the *temple of flesh*, the
wages of sin, the *lake of fire*, and which entertained me
until I realised none of it made sense any more. I was in
a bed wearing an orthopaedic corset, a nurse wiped my
backside every day, and what position of authority was I
in from which to take anyone else for a fool? How could
I place myself above them? The performance I gave at
the eleven o'clock meetings until the eve of the Nirvana
show, without ever having believed in the Bible, in the
Church of the Plenitude, in the prophets, in Jesus
Christ, in God or in anything else but myself, now
sounded every bit as ridiculous as trying to hide that
condition – who I was in that hospital, what had happened in that year.

Whenever I hear believers tell their stories, there's
always a moment when they say they've reached rock
bottom. It's when something makes you confess. Makes

you accept the revelation on your knees, you embrace the faith, a new life or whatever name you give it. I can't say that was how it was in the hospital, because what comes in the gaps between meals, the drawing of blood, the miniature TV that I never switched on, is not despair so much as tedium. What motivated me wasn't a miracle either, but when I heard the lieutenant's account of his conversion, as he explained how good it was to be saved, how good it was to be alive and to see the beauty in things, even that white wall, even those plastic flowers, and how even the pain of the operating theatre and of the ICU and of the isolation ward are signs of a life trying to sustain itself until the final breath – when I heard his account it made me feel a kind of tiredness, a surrender mixed with months of distress, the lieutenant sitting by the bed, the last time we met, the goodbye because I knew I wouldn't be going back to the barracks after the accident, and we wouldn't be friends after it was all over, and in spite of everything he was the person closest to understanding what I was going through, and I had nothing more to lose anyway, and so I looked at the lieutenant and for the first time told him the whole story of Valéria.

74.

The second time I told the whole story was at a meeting with Alexandre. I decided to seek him out once I had recovered from the accident. It wasn't hard: I knew his full name and that he was studying at the state university. It's strange making the call, introducing yourself, saying you'd like to meet the guy to talk about an ex-girlfriend he surely wanted to forget. Valéria was sixteen when the two of them had seen each other last, another reason why my meeting with him seemed so late, months after the Nirvana show. My first question was about the reason the relationship had ended, I need a few details, I'm sorry, and he knew that I knew that his answer would only make things worse.

At sixteen Valéria looked at the blue of a vein in her wrist. She was in the bathroom, at Alexandre's house, holding a kitchen knife. I imagine the hot water running in the sink, as she thought what would happen if she made a little cut, half a centimetre, a little more pressure, the skin folding inward and then how long before the red would rise out behind the thick steam, a shapeless cloud that grew slowly and in every direction as if proving there is something inside you that's alive.

It's easy to look at Valéria's story as a mirror of her mother's, as though she had no autonomy to escape a plotline scripted by the crappiest of psychology text-books. Alexandre told me what had happened shortly before she went into the bathroom, the conversation where he'd said he felt trapped, that it didn't make sense carrying on with the relationship, that he had to be honest because of how special she was. Valéria's first kiss was Alexandre. The first guy she slept with was him. Her first big disappointment after her mother's death happened on that day. The bathroom was on the second floor of his parents' house, and for some reason Alexandre couldn't remember Valéria didn't leave at the end of the conversation. For some reason he saw nothing wrong when she said she needed to wash her face. For some reason he let her lock the bathroom door, staying there for what seemed a ridiculous length of time, the act of filling the sink and keeping her hands in there for several minutes, before he knocked on the door and called out to her a few times. There was no need to break it down because the house had a master key that opened every room. When he came in, Valéria was on the floor, conscious, but she looked at him as though she did not recognise him.

75.

Alexandre's parents weren't home. He called for an ambulance and he didn't even need to carry Valéria. She didn't cry and she didn't resist as she lay down on the stretcher. The incident ended up not being too serious because the cut was perpendicular to the vein, not parallel. Valéria had given no indication that she might do such a thing, or at least none that Alexandre had noticed, nothing apart from the crying and the silence after she had calmed down, nothing apart from what any sixteen-year-old girl is capable of after the end of a relationship. I can only guess what she felt as she turned on the tap, the water level gradually rising, as she took the knife from her bag as though there were someone there, Alexandre, Valéria's mother, and never letting go of it while saying just look how well I can keep on going without asking for help.

I can only guess that her behaviour was typical of her and independent of others, that whether it was me or Alexandre or anybody else, it wouldn't have made any difference because the story would have had the same outcome. They say it is never a surprise. That the act is never unplanned. The person who commits it spends months busily pretending in front of their family and friends, and during that time pretends in various ways whatever it is they intend to appear deliberate or not. This is reflected in the choice of method, in the clues left behind, in any words written in the preceding days and weeks in the event of there not being a proper note.

Valéria's postcard was the only clue to how she was feeling in São Paulo. Everything else I only learned because Nail told me, in a meeting like the one I had with Alexandre, except this time it was not on my initiative. It was Nail who insisted on seeing me. We met in a coffee shop on Fernandes Vieira, the week after Hollywood Rock. I can describe the coffee shop: a hamburger grill, the noise of the blender making juice, me in the bathroom washing my hands and wondering whether I really wanted to have this conversation. If not, it was just a matter of drying myself off, going back out to the main room, walking without a glance right past the table where Nail was waiting for me as though it were an encounter just like any other, my last chance to do what? To throw a fourth punch at him? To ask if he's tried the vanilla milkshake cos the one they do here is really good?

76.

Nail told me about the São Paulo bus station, about going to the post office on the Friday morning, about him and Valéria in a square close to the Morumbi on the Saturday waiting for the flow to abate after the show was done. While he talked I paid closer attention: the way he turned over his plate, the way he straightened out the cutlery, the clothes he'd chosen, a pair of jeans and trainers that might have been the same ones he'd worn at the Nirvana show. I checked whether there was mud on the trainers, whether they retained any vestige of the night that for some reason he felt obliged to tell me about: a moment after I returned from the bathroom he was already talking about the trees on the square, the lighting, about how the Morumbi was a trap it was impossible to get out of in less than forty minutes, the narrow streets and the cars and the crowds on the pavements while the waiter handed us the menu and stood there waiting for him to shut up and get on and order something once and for all.

What Nail drank: a coffee. What Nail ate: a pasty. Then, another pasty. I drank my vanilla milkshake in silence, without looking at the glass. I didn't ask Nail for any additional explanations. I didn't ask why he was telling me all this. I didn't look at him, and, my voice calm, after a pause to make it absolutely clear who was in a position to be judging whom, me and Nail sitting there now, and ever since the dance with Sandra right up to that meeting, almost a decade coming to an end at that crumb-covered table, and the last time I saw him chewing and wiping his mouth as if I hadn't noticed who he was and what he deserved, I didn't look at him and didn't say what I should have said. He seemed to want me to say it. I think that was why he invited me there. Except it no longer mattered: when the waiter brought the bill we had already been sitting in silence for some time, Nail clean-shaven, the television switched to an Afternoon Movie, a scene in which someone was on a train journey during a snowstorm, and what did the setting matter and how long was the gap between waiting for our change and me getting up and Nail doing the same, the two of us out on the street and I must have said bye and he said bye and each of us went off in our own direction knowing we'd never see each other again?

77·

The first time Valéria inhaled ethyl chloride, *perfume spray* as they call it here, was on a friend's sofa. The sensation of an icy handkerchief gives way to the noise of a siren and a prickling of sweet gas, which makes you feel your muscles stretching euphorically. She always knew how at that moment the heart beats, pressure rises and for a moment you can't tell if your body is ready to take the hit. Every time you inhale it again it's like you're accepting that doubt, putting your reaction in the hands of destiny or your genes, and I can remember at least two conversations with Valéria when she said that was the one drug she really couldn't do. It's the only one that scares me, she said. That makes me feel like I'm losing control. Like I'm about to die.

Valéria went into cardiac arrest less than an hour after the Nirvana show, in the square close to the Morumbi, barely twenty-four hours after I'd chosen to pay Diogo rather than get on the plane. After I'd promised Diogo I'd get the money the following week. After I'd decided to return my plane ticket, sell my ticket to the gig via another friend who was going to São Paulo, save what I'd put aside for travelling expenses, all of it in exchange for not going to prison and losing my first girlfriend.

Friday at the barracks was sunny, and I took my lesson in dismantling a rifle while eight hundred and fifty kilometres away my first girlfriend was walking into the post office. I separated the lower receiver while she stuck the stamp onto the postcard. I pulled out the bolt carrier assembly while she paid at the till, then I separated the firing pin, the bolt cam pin, the extractor pin, and to this day I don't know whether the lyrics on the postcard were merely innocent quotes from an innocent song or a message. I don't know if her tone was that from the beginning of the relationship or the more recent one, an irony that had sounded innocent when I didn't know Valéria all that well or from today's more unsettled mood. I don't know whether Valéria knew that Nail would have a bottle of perfume spray on the day of the show, whether she told him that something might happen when she inhaled once, twice, fifteen times, however many times were necessary on that square, like a lottery, until that bottle was empty and Nail would be able to take advantage of the moment to do what, to give Valéria a kiss? And hadn't he done that already, anyway?

I don't know where Nail got hold of the perfume

spray, if it was his idea or hers, if it was him or her who first accepted it when someone offered. It's strange to think that with all the drugs available in 1993 someone should have got hold of something so obsolete, a souvenir of the Carnivals of the fifties. It was hard to find: a trip to Uruguay, a casino, a sumptuous cut of dripping meat and two hundred kilometres on a straight, green road where you buy cheese and *doce de leite* and maybe the border guards happen to search your car, where you have an infinite amount of time to weigh up whether it is worth risking your life just to have Valéria's face pressed against yours, Valéria's mouth, the two of you beneath the tree in a square where I've never been and will never be, Nail's perfect plan while I slept in Porto Alegre satisfied at having exchanged my chance to avoid such an outcome, for what I thought would be thirty days of freedom.

78.

One baby to another says
I'm lucky to have met you
I don't care what you think
Unless it is about me

With eyes so dilated
I've become your pupil
You've taught me everything
With a poison apple

79.

I don't know where Valéria learned English. I guess it was in one of those classes where you spend years talking to the teacher and you can't understand two lines of a movie without subtitles. I don't know how long you need to take a class like that before you learn the difference between *with* and *without,* to know that the lyrics really said you've taught me everything *without* a poison apple.

I don't know whether Valéria understood the biblical reference that Kurt Cobain kind of denied, the idea that in order to attain knowledge you've got to pay some kind of price, the most banal kind of romanticism if we replace *knowledge* with *the sublime* and *price* with *suffering,* and yet I also don't know whether the mix-up was deliberate, whether she left Porto Alegre actually planning to write the postcard with the lyrics wrong, and whether with that actual intention in mind, she rejected the standard mail, she didn't want to use registered post, she didn't even consider the express couriers because there was a service that offered a guaranteed delivery date and with this, instead of the three working days which would mean I'd read it on the Wednesday or Thursday after the show, she scheduled it for two months later, on my birthday, as if it were a belated bouquet of flowers or perfume or a box of chocolates appearing under the door.

80.

About eight in the evening on my birthday, two months after Valéria's death, I arrived home and found no one there. My father was at work, my mother had gone out, the maid left at four and I wasn't out of the barracks till half past six and got on a first bus downtown and a second over to my neighbourhood. I took my cap, my off-duty tie and combats out of my rucksack, ironed my trousers and polished my combat boots so as not to have to do it the following day, hung the clothes on two hangers and the hangers on two doorknobs, and only then did I look at the kitchen floor and see there was something under the door. My *box of chocolates*. Then I recognised the handwriting on the postcard, and for a moment I couldn't tell whether it was some kind of trick or an ancient piece of correspondence that by some error was being delivered so late.

In the eleven months I spent with Valéria, I never guessed at anything like the story with Alexandre and the bathroom and the ambulance. They say these things go in cycles, that a person can go for years living perfectly functionally. Perhaps I'd known Valéria in just such a period, an interval in which she lived normally knowing that at any moment and for any reason her balance could tip upside down. That in some way she was waiting for this, the pretext she'd anticipated the Friday before the show, with me and Nail and Kurt Cobain in supporting roles in the drama that was only ever hers, a girl from Porto Alegre, 1993, whom I met by chance in a bar in Independência, and who happened to become my first girlfriend, and it's so easy to believe those links were formed with no interference from anybody else, and I had no way of guessing how it'd turn out, a story that wasn't even as unusual as all that, just a mistake that can happen, the stroke of bad luck that everybody gets from time to time, finding yourself faced with neurosis, madness, the selfishness of someone who leaves other people with a bill that will never be paid in full.

81.

Did Courtney Love forgive Kurt Cobain? Did Frances Bean ever think that her father did what he did because it was inevitable? I picture Valéria at the post office, waiting for other people to finish sending off their parcels and documents, asking the clerk about fixed-date home delivery. I don't know whether the delivery is set at the till or at a special counter for that kind of service, where she fills in a form, pays a fee, retrieves her change. I don't know whether with each of these meticulous actions Valéria wondered whether I deserved to be put through this, whether what I had done was really as terrible as all that, an eighteen-year-old student who didn't want to give any quarter in an argument, who didn't know how to handle his first girlfriend, and was too proud to admit he was jealous of his best friend, and took advantage of the excuse of the barracks and Diogo and the pot to bring forward a decision that he might be making anyway.

82.

I keep wondering what Immaculée Ilibagiza must think of someone like Kurt Cobain. After our conversation in São Paulo I even imagined an interview in which she commented on each line in his farewell note. *There's good in all of us and I think I simply love people too much*: tell me, Ms Ilibagiza, do you feel some solidarity with the dramas faced by the author of these words? *Sometimes I feel as if I should have a punch-in time clock before I walk out on stage*: would you agree that it's too great a burden for the author? *The worst crime I can think of would be to rip people off by faking it and pretending as if I'm having 100 per cent fun*: what do you think of the author having written this part a day before the war began in Rwanda?

83.

I keep wondering whether Valéria would consider someone like Immaculée her great idol. And whether it's also a coincidence that she happened to come across a badly recorded tape of Nirvana or whether it would have happened anyway, and if it wasn't Kurt Cobain it would have been another one of those sensitive artist types, those turbulent souls. There's always a price to be paid by someone who finds beauty by confronting his inner demons, and any record made in thirty days sounds like an epic understanding of the hostile universe because the artist describes the labour pains of creating those melodies and lyrics, the posture and the final destination that are so common in the history of pop music because there's always someone prepared to see themselves as in tune with that martyrdom. I keep imagining an interview with Valéria in which she comments line by line on Immaculée's book. *I was the living proof of the power of prayer and positive thinking*: does that line sound naïve to you, Valéria? *He left me to tell my story to others and show as many people as possible the healing power of His love and forgiveness*: do you find this bit tacky, Valéria? *The love of a single heart can make a world of difference*: was there any purpose to this woman having been through such a fundamental experience, Valéria, if at the end of it all she does is give a wishy-washy lesson in tackiness in a lecture aimed at goody-two-shoes and nuns?

84.

Suicide is a medical problem, a religious, philo-sophical, moral and legal problem. There are statistics on the relation to illnesses, social disintegration, drug abuse and the influence of other suicides in a chain reaction, hence the school of thought that favours not releasing cases to the press and the care that should be taken with those people in the suicide's close circle because it is not uncommon for a relative to take inspir-ation from the dead person's example.

Suicide is a betrayal of others and of oneself, of what you might become in future, a different person who can never exist because the thread was broken before the mistakes could be corrected. If the inter-viewer had been Valéria and I the interviewee, the dialogue would be limited to the words of 1993. She could not ask me questions with any knowledge beyond what she had at the time. Valéria would ask: *do you really believe in this business of the glamour of illness? Have you ever asked the mother of a schizo-phrenic whether she'd prefer her son to have a bladder complaint?*

85

Have you ever asked someone in a wheelchair if their life really is over? Have you ever looked at a blind person, with serious burns? Someone who survived eight doses of chemotherapy at twelve years old? So many people who wake up and learn before lunch that they have less than three months left to live. Have you noticed whether the person has family and friends? If up until the last minute you might want to do something other than think about what you reckon she is thinking? What authority do you have to speculate about these people? Have you been in their skin? Have you spoken to anyone close to them? Did you know anything beyond what you read in the newspapers you so like to criticise, written by those journalists who are so far beneath you? Or during a fifteen-minute conversation with the tape recorder on? How you do judge what a wife feels about her husband? Or what a daughter feels about her father? Or what an addict feels about himself? Or what a woman who has lost it all feels about anything?

86.

Valéria's voice in my memory will always have that tone to it, what it was possible to know before the Nirvana show, to say or not to say. If I lined her questions up they'd form a list of twenty, ninety, five hundred ways of requiring that an eighteen-year-old assure his first girlfriend whom he'd met eleven months earlier that he would never leave her.

I could argue that I was actually dealing with two cases of blackmail: I left the eleven o'clock meeting on Friday, looked for Diogo in the classroom, in the billets, on the athletics track, and sorted out the business with the money because it was a way of surrendering to the lesser of two evils. At least with him I'd have some practical advantage, unlike what would happen if I paid the price demanded by Valéria in going to São Paulo. It's so easy to confuse the weariness of being eleven months into a relationship with what I felt when I passed through the barracks gate that Friday. It's so easy to think of it as a relief. To think I had already lived through enough of Valéria's highs and lows. That it was time to put an end to it, and how many times had I fantasised about just this opportunity, to get free of the neuroses, the peace of turning my back on Valéria, a decision taken in ten seconds and a problem that instantaneously disappears and you realise you have the rest of your life ahead of you.

It's so easy to put the choice into an order that is almost physical, like when somebody throws themselves onto a child who is about to be attacked by a dog, or steps in front of an attacker and takes a bullet for a friend, or does the opposite of this and says it was instinct rather than morality, more inertia than will, a response to circumstances that are experienced by each of us differently. Nobody who hasn't gone through basic training at the CPOR is in a position to judge, and so the conversation with Diogo becomes less compromising than it seems and I do what anybody would do in my place. I find Diogo at the door to the billets, both of us standing in the sun, thirty-three degrees at five minutes past noon on Friday, the look on his face when he accepts my offer of scheduling the payment into four instalments over a hundred and twenty days, during which time I would manage to get the refund for my flight and the Nirvana ticket. I would put aside a portion of my future earnings, I'd figure out a way of getting hold of the rest, and he could trust me because I've never failed to keep a promise and I've never let anyone down.

87.

And things could have ended there, with Valéria just the first girlfriend with whom I lost touch. I would come to talk about her in the resigned tone of someone commenting on a list that began at the age of eighteen: a doctor – I met her when I returned from England – and then an architecture student soon afterwards, all the women I met and each of whom taught me something. I could have gone on to explain that at the end of each relationship you feel sad and you feel you have no strength left, but the time comes when you've got to start looking forward. That is when the phases of rebirth are finally completed, which in my case will always be mirrored by the departure from the barracks on that Friday, feeling relieved that I would never have to think about Valéria again because the consequences would be experienced in a city eight hundred and fifty kilometres away. With any luck she wouldn't seek me out when she got back from São Paulo, and I wouldn't have to justify myself in those endless conversations, an analysis I was no longer inclined to undergo since throwing those punches at Nail, a new phase without arguments and relapses and the responsibility for taking care of someone in a state of constant hysteria. Then there was the rest of the afternoon, the Saturday, the Sunday morning, the hour in which I still had a hope of becoming that person I could no longer be after the phone rang and I answered and I recognised Nail's voice and he said he had some news to tell me.

88.

You love thinking you came out of this story a different person. The survivor who learned a lesson. And you were marked by how much this tough life screws us over, isn't that right? You want someone to be impressed by a few months in the barracks, is that it? A few months waking up early, ironing your uniform, just imagine! Shaving properly. A few months playing at having a band. The only person in the world who ever had a car accident. Two months in bed, and then the sultan in exile. You know the names of the streets in London, is that it? You went to the museums and parks? You used the Tube and woke early to go to work, really it's some adventure. And then you came back to your mummy's house. And finished college. And went off to be a journalist in São Paulo. And for the rest of your life you thought you'd had, as they say, quite the youth.

You've seen forty now. A disillusioned man. The sage who grants other people pity but doesn't miss a chance to make the most of the pity that appears in so many ways in exchange. What an interesting guy he is. Mystery is always charming. How many years will he continue to live suspended in a plot that concerns someone who is no longer here? Someone who will never be able to defend herself. The stereotype of the unpredictable, undecipherable woman. The crazy girl who ruined the past of this poor middle-aged man in a crisis. That's what matters, isn't that right? Whether or not you suffered. What you think of the story. When at no point in the story do you say what you felt at the moment when you made the decision. What you really felt in those eleven months. You who had a life so filled with adventures, and did you ever have the most important experience of all? Did you ever really get involved with something? Did you ever really like someone? Did you make a sacrifice for another person? Give up something of value? Offer any proof? Have you been willing to lose just once? I mean really lose,

without the compensation of victimhood. Just you and
your defeat. You and the end. Just the end. Nothing else
and no one else, only the end.

89.

Valéria's body arrived by plane, on the Tuesday.
Mourning can be experienced in many ways, and for
me it began at the CPOR: the world didn't stop because
of me, there was the power of the barracks to transform
everything into repetition, the bugle, the anthem, the
flag, the parade, the changing block, the card they use
to keep track of our haircuts. If I hadn't been serving in
1993, hadn't needed to be in shape every morning, my
body ready for the duties that stopped me from thinking about what had been or what might have been, and
had just lain prostrate on a bed, utterly prevented from
moving forward by the kind of regret that saps away
your strength till you can barely lift a spoon – might I
have done immediately what is expected in such cases,
and sunk into a spiral of paralysing sadness?

I completed basic training without talking to anyone in the platoon about Valéria. I did my tests and
came seventy-first out of the two hundred students of

the CPOR, high enough to get a position doing desk duty and spend the rest of the year taking it easier, dedicating myself to learning about storage, transport, administrative and budgetary controls, all without using Valéria's name as an excuse. If someone were watching from the outside, they'd say it was as though her death had never happened. And filling the working days with as many activities as possible was a way of turning the page on everything connected to the episode, Nail, the guitar I never played again, the funeral I refused to attend.

If someone were watching from the outside all they'd see would be the autopilot of opening my eyes, getting out of bed, putting on my uniform, tying my combat boots, putting a pot of water on to boil and making coffee, opening the fridge to get some butter to spread on the bread before leaving the house every morning, each movement so natural for someone who's eighteen years old and has no physical ailment, a body that needs nourishing, cleaning, tiring out, hydrating and being restored each day, the survival instinct that makes every person keep on moving forward despite everything, but of course everything is not simply moving forward in accordance with this instinct.

90.

I was detached from the army two months later, because of the accident. I went into the reserves as a Category 3, the same as someone who has got an exemption from enlistment due to an oversupply of conscripts. I never wore a uniform again, nor studied the Bible, nor attended any evangelical ceremony or group or had the curiosity to do any research into what Christianity, Judaism, Islam or any religion says or doesn't say about mourning, free will, forgiveness.

91.

I have been to London a few times since 1994, and even by the first of these visits the coffee shop was no longer there. The hostel where I'd lived had been renovated. I never heard anything else about my boss, about the Spaniard who shared my room, about the job agent and the people whose paths I crossed during that year, and the city has so changed with the whole economic boom and the Olympics and the newly done-up neighbourhoods and new museums and buildings and tourist attractions that today I barely recognise any of it.

92.

Immaculée Ilibagiza's life inspired a film that was announced by the producer of *The Passion of the Christ*. I don't know if she'll become an actual celebrity, a superstar of survival beyond the realm of lectures financed by Catholic bodies, nor if the film will premiere before or after the twentieth anniversary of Kurt Cobain's death, in April 2014. I don't intend to see it, nor read the articles about the anniversary, nor learn what became of Courtney Love and Frances Bean, of Nail and Felicien, of Alexandre and of the friend who sold my Nirvana ticket, nor to speak of the jobs I've had and the things I've done or any of the characters and facts which like everything that came after are a part of this story, too.

93.

I don't want to go back and talk about the two months between the news I received from Nail and my birthday. Valéria's death will never cease to be a mystery, and the postcard might have been merely something that just occurred to her when she was walking past the post office. The ironic tone of the beginning of our relationship or that other tone, the one which twenty years on has come to sound like a premonition? A note like Kurt Cobain's or the simulation of a farewell closely resembling melodrama, as she had already tried jokingly so many times before: what will you say when you hear I've died? Will you speak at my funeral? What will you wear? Who's going to be invited?

I never again heard anything of Valéria's father, nor of her friends and acquaintances, and perhaps I'm the only person who still remembers certain details today, the questions she used to ask only me and that alter this storyline only for me: the possible chance event that would seem to explain the outcome that begins when I pay Diogo. I say again the relationship really didn't have a future, and I would have left Valéria anyway because she was an unstable person, an infinite source of problems I didn't need to face so early on, and anybody in my position would have taken advantage of the opportunity not to go to São Paulo and to end it all painlessly.

It's so easy to convince oneself that was how it happened. I've almost forgotten what it was like the rest of the time: which memories I keep and which I don't, which lines of Valéria's do I choose, and it falls to me alone to judge the weight of the last ten minutes of the eighteen years of her life, whether what happened in those ten minutes was premeditated or just an accident, if the craziness I could see in her really existed to the degree I imagined or if it was just a small flaw, like when we notice that our friends aren't quite as honest as they might be, as smart, as generous.

It falls to me alone to judge whether Valéria was the person who came into the world to destroy me or just a girl from Porto Alegre, 1993, who compensated for her insecurity using the one thing she had at her disposal, the only weapon she had in those arguments that could easily be used as proof that she was the only unbalanced one. And then I forget the days when there weren't arguments, that other tone of voice, her whispering in my ear just don't think I haven't noticed. That I don't know you feel the same way about me. Beneath your pride. Admit it, just once, tell me at least once.

94.

In 'Drain You', one of the babies tells the other his duty is to drain her completely, extract her individual essence. Cancel out the other person until she becomes you and you cancel yourself out to become the other person, too, and how many people go through their lives without experiencing anything like it? When I talk about Valéria it would be ridiculous to remember what existed beyond this basic doubt, because it's obvious that we did also have what you'd consider the day-to-day life of a couple, chats about the rain and sun and electric dryer and gas bill, a Sunday morning reading the paper in bed, the batteries for the remote control, the smell of food at home.

Memories of a relationship can also be summarised into not much, a trip, a bike ride, the writing on a T-shirt, secret nicknames and in-jokes which make sense only to two people, a dictionary of feelings and the museum of a phase of life, but none of this matters compared with what Valéria meant. Her favourite meal doesn't matter. The movies she liked watching don't matter. It doesn't matter the way she used to cough, how she stretched, the way her legs moved when she walked, the shape of her nails and the taste of her mouth at various times of day, the sounds, the smell, the little obsessions, the predictable reactions and the unpredictable ones, because it's as though my memory exists now to explain not her past, which was buried on the day of the Nirvana show, but the future of the part that survived: who I really am, the question I've been asking myself since 1993, the things I did and the people I met and the decisions made in an existence which has been predictable but for one single exception.

95.

Like Valéria, I enjoy red meat, fried eggs, Middle Eastern food. My favourite movie in 1993 was *Goodfellas*. My cough is drier than hers because I've never been a cigarette smoker. She went to bed late and woke late, and I'm the opposite. Her nails were straight at the tips, and I remember the taste of cool beer, or coffee, or when she came back to bed and kissed me and I could taste the sweetness of the toothpaste and it was a good way to start the day. She wore vanilla perfume, she put on a little kiddie voice when she said she had a cold, and whenever I was sick or feeling down she would do anything to make me better. She'd heat up the soup, offer to go to the chemist's to buy medicine, think up any pretext to get me out of the house. There were weeks when we never argued once, and on my birthday before the one in 1993 she spent a load of money she didn't have to give me a shirt and a dinner and a CD player.

96.

Valéria came to my parents' apartment three times. The first, when she didn't make it inside, was the incident with the screaming that woke the neighbourhood. On the second, they were out. On the third I introduced her briefly, a conversation which lasted no more than two minutes, my mother offering some water or an ice cream and Valéria saying thanks. In the eleven months we spent together she didn't meet one of my classmates from college. None of the students from the CPOR. I told her only generalities about the law firm, my childhood, the first band I had with Nail, and I don't remember a single occasion when we discussed living together, and I couldn't say whether or not she liked children and whether there was a future planned in which I was forty years old and every night we had dinner with the TV on. I don't know whether those twenty years would have made her know me better. I don't know whether I would have changed all that much if she were still alive. Valéria didn't introduce me to her father, or show me photos of him or of any relative, and I don't remember where she was studying, or the names of those friends I was introduced to, and there are so many things I don't know about her and she didn't know about me, and in spite of this in the things that matter no people are more alike than we two.

97.

Like me, Valéria didn't believe in God. At least I never heard her utter the word. I never heard her defend a party, a cause, an idea with any conviction beyond a banal argument about the town hall tarmacking the roads on the outskirts of the city or the killer of a soap actress deserving more years in prison. There was nothing unusual in this from day to day, the neutral surface of the lives of people who also go to the bank and take the bus and at eighteen consider sitting the college entrance exam in communications, there was a whole part of her life that was not so determined, intense, a kind of extremism she kept exclusively for certain conversations and certain reactions she had to certain attitudes of mine.

Valéria once asked me, how long after I'm buried will you miss me? What will you miss about me the most, how will you live without me? And it's so easy to forget that had always been there. And that she liked talking to me at the bar in Independência because I played guitar, or because I listened to the same bands, or because of my laugh, or some physical quality that I can't begin to imagine, and not because someone like her can scent the presence of somebody like me from far away. Someone who would reply to each one of those questions in turn. And is able to go all the way in order to answer them. And then you try to make it happen, and try every trick in the book to make the person reveal herself, what is purest in her, her essence, her truth.

The memory of a relationship can be a song, a refrain, the banal sequence of E minor, A, B minor and full-tone D of 'Drain You', and you do not choose to have your entire life linked to eight lines from some stupid guy who shot himself in the head more than twenty years ago. You don't choose to be linked to someone who did something stupid twenty years ago, and never again will the identification with any other person be so intense, the stupidity that's also yours and the illness that's also in you, the awareness of that limit that isn't a limit because you were able at least once to transcend it.

98.

Which part of me will you miss the most? Which part of you makes me like you most? Not the worst part, it's easy to know what that is. You have yours, I have mine, but that's not the only thing I see in you and you see in me. Because I know how you think. What you expect of me. I look at you and it's like seeing myself in the mirror. The same features. The same expression up close. Then you look back at me and my face is yours now, the nose, the colour of the skin, the neck and the rest of the body and I close my eyes and focus on what's inside this anatomy, the cells and the lungs breathing and the heart beating and how fragile the body is and for your whole life it runs like clockwork until the moment when the gears jam just before you hurt yourself.

What is it to like someone? How do you know you like them if this doesn't turn into something you actually do? A proof. Even just once. And for the rest of your life you know. You spent your life in ignorance, in the limbo of solitude and tedium and now there's no way back. Just ask and I'll show you. As though it were an altar to you. I'll make a little cut in my wrist, and do you feel it, too? I tear off a little piece of flesh. A finger. My whole arm. Both legs, and will you also tear off yours? It's so easy not to think about the pain, isn't it? Not to think about the act. To be left only with what comes after, truly merging into another person, and when we feel this at the same time it's possible to increase the intensity of the charge, closer, stronger, greater than I can bear and you can bear, and I say yes and my bones and my veins and the air that isn't enough and you say yes and the world doesn't matter because everything comes down to this, on this night when time stops and no one will ever part us.

99.

At some point in the ninety-one days she spent in the bathroom, Immaculée Ilibagiza realised her only chance would be a UN intervention. The soldiers who could free her would speak English, and she needed to know the bare minimum of the language to explain to them and to the world who she was and what had happened. The pastor had a dictionary in the house, half a dozen books that had come from England, and she convinced him to give up the books because it was another way of telling the liberators about how he had saved her life despite being a Hutu.

Immaculée studied alone, on her feet, in silence, her elbows resting against the backs of the other women, sensing by trial and error what were nouns, verbs, adverbs and adjectives hidden in a code that was then still mysterious, and this willpower, also attributed to divine Providence, is one of the lessons to which she often refers. I heard lesson after lesson in the lecture at PUC, sitting in the second row of the auditorium, and that was the moment I began to compare her story with Kurt Cobain's: whether there was also something to be drawn from his final moments, the translation he also had to carry out with his final note, the code for explaining the reason he was in that place and on that day with that gun in his hand.

The last thing Kurt Cobain ever smelled was cooked heroin. The last thing he tasted was beer mixed with tobacco. The last thing he saw was the linoleum floor which had been chosen because it was easy to clean. He left his ID card face up so that he would be easily recognised by whoever found him. The dawn was breaking, time to ask forgiveness and say farewell, and what does the tragedy of this person, summarised today into a few dozen photographs and footage of shows and studio recordings, like the tragedy of that woman from Rwanda and so many other tragedies I have forgotten or never known, what does it teach me about the tragedy that really does interest me and always has?

When I ask myself Valéria's questions, imitating for my own benefit the way I imagine she would be speaking them, it's not just the voice from twenty years back that I'm summoning up. It's not just her uncertainties, but the answers frozen in time. Those I was able to give, back then. I summon up my own voice, too, knowing that I'm speaking the way I spoke one night in 1993, to Valéria and to myself, the pact agreed with no other witnesses. Time to ask forgiveness and say farewell: it's from this that you do not return, the code that stops being mysterious when you have the courage to use it, the one word you were looking for, the first time you use it and discover that this one word is what you feel and what you are.

100.

You knew it would end like this, didn't you? I
spent two months pretending I didn't, as though hiding
from other people was the same as hiding from myself.
The state I was in from the moment I heard the news,
what I thought from that first minute, then sixty days
when it was so easy to abstract myself in practical chores,
wake up at the right time, go where they ask me to go, do
what they tell me – because this thought is always there,
always available above it all, the offer you made me
and which could not be ignored. I was not going to disap-
point you. I was not going to abandon you. I have never
abandoned you, and twenty years on this remains true.

101.

It was an autumn night, but cold. At eight the rain
lets up in Porto Alegre, the headlamps leave a red trace
where your tired eyes stare at the void, and you arrive
home and take off your cap and tie and iron your trousers and polish your combat boots as though it were the
most urgent thing you needed to do on your birthday.

I could go on summarising that night as a succession

of little tasks, as though the effect of finding the postcard could be cancelled out by the routine. But the
actions were different in their nature now: I put the
card in my pocket, called the lift again, started up my
mother's car which I sometimes borrowed, drove over
to a bar where I used to go with my platoon friends on
Fridays. I was alone, I drank a toast to Valéria and to
myself, nineteen years all done, when the barman
brought the first of the six caipirinhas I drank.

The accident happened because of the drink, the
trip to London because of the accident, the change in
profession because of the trip to London, the departure
from Porto Alegre because of the change in profession,
and the things I did and the person I became because
of all of this, and what else can be drawn out of a biography that was initiated by those eight lines in my
pocket? The moment when everything became so
clear: the two months between the Nirvana show and
that night, with me deluding myself it wouldn't be like
that, sixty days in which I pretended Valéria had no
right to this, her final wish, the proof she had always
wanted and which was now within my reach.

I paid the bill at the bar after the sixth caipirinha, and
this was what I had to offer Valéria. I got up and felt dizzy

and ready and it was what I was able to say at that moment: look, Valéria, the way I'm walking because of you. How I bump into the next table. And stagger out to the car park. And turn the key. And go on as far as Protásio Alves in your honour, look how the light's red, thirty seconds waiting and I will be able to go back home and sleep and life will go on just the same because in four decades I won't have truly committed myself to anything.

So many things to explain a vocation, a destiny, a personality, and sometimes it's so much easier to summarise everything into the hesitation at that traffic light: did I or did I not see the fire engine. Did I or did I not calculate that there would be a crash as I ran the light. Did it happen or was it like a dream, a night-time delirium in which, for the first time, I thought in those terms, when for the first time I used that word, a fraction of a second and everything to lose in the name of the one person who got me to say it. Everything that happened afterwards and none of it will compare to this. I met so many people, and no one else was able to tear this from me. And it's then, as the proof I owed you in return, you who have finally brought me to this point, the mark you left and which will never be removed, my love, it's then that I ask you if I should step on the gas.